Redeeming Holy Rock

Book 12

"My Son's Wife" series

"Perfect Stories About Imperfect People
Like You...and Me"

Redeeming Holy Rock

Book 12

"My Son's Wife" series

NATIONAL BESTSELLING AUTHOR

Shelia E. Bell

ISBN: 978-1-7355432-8-4

Library of Congress Control Number: 2022905071

This is a work of fiction. Any references or similarities to actual events, real people living, or dead, or to real locales are intended to give the novel a sense of reality. Any similarity in other names, characters, places, and incidents is purely coincidental.

Back cover metadata courtesy of Eve Alexander

www.sheliawritebooks.com
Aurora, Colorado

Dedication

To all literary supporters who have made this series of characters come alive and stay alive, forcing me to keep moving in my God given talents and gifts.

Acknowledgements

"Everyone needs a support system, be it family, friends, coworkers, therapists, or religious leaders. We cannot do life alone and expect to keep mentally, emotionally, and spiritually healthy. Everyone needs some sort of support system on which to rely." R. E. Goodrich

I want to take this moment and acknowledge **YOU!** Yes I'm talking about **YOU.** The ones who continue to push me to do what I have been called to do. I thank God for blessing me with the gift to imagine. I thank Him for motivating me to keep going even when I have tried to talk myself out of doing what I know I have been chosen to do, which is write. I thank Him for placing the right people along my path and removing the wrong people out of my way so I can keep pressing forward. I am eternally grateful to each reader, to every book club, to my social media followers, to my beta readers, my editor, and any and everyone who supports my work. I'm always thankful and grateful to my family and friends.

Love y'all so much

Shelia E. Bell
God's Amazing Girl

one

"It takes two people to create a successful relationship. It only takes one person to make it fail." Unknown

Rianna sat across from Stiles with her long shapely coffee brown legs crossed, and her red A-line dress seductively showcasing peaks of her voluptuous brown mounds and resting at her upper thighs.

"You know what, I can't believe you. You parade up in here with your outrageous demands while my brother is rotting away in prison for the next twenty years! You have some nerves. And to add insult to injury," Stiles fumed, "when was the last time you visited him?"

Stiles stared at his sister-in-law. Her arched brows and red glossy lipstick screamed perfection. Her flawless makeup may have shouted beauty but it was laced with ugly—a devil in a red dress. He pulled away and focused on the dwarf sitting in the chair next to her. "And who is this you say you brought with you?"

"I told you, His name is Abel...Abel Cane. He's my financial consultant. And for your information, I just came from seeing my husband a few days ago. Not that I have to report to you," she retorted, rolling her eyes and huffing.

Abel nodded but remained tight-lipped. Rianna was handling herself quite well, something he was more than used to seeing her do. She could make the most confident person squirm. Her brother-in-law seemed to take no exception.

"Well, anyway, I don't appreciate you barging into my office unannounced and bringing some stranger along with you, especially to talk about my brother's personal affairs."

"I told you, Abel is my finance guy *and* a personal friend," she barked, slinging her burgundy waist-length lace front away from her face. "But to be honest, I don't see why you would be bothered about that. Anyway, back to the reason I'm here. I told you weeks ago what my intentions were."

"And I'm telling you the same thing I told you then," he snarled, "you must be out of your mind. No way would I ever turn this church over to you. What is wrong with you?" He frowned, picked up an ink pen, and nervously started tapping it on his solid wood desktop. "My brother worked too hard to start this church and I will not sit back while you make a mockery of his dreams and everything God has called him to do."

Rianna rose to her feet, pivoting back and forth on her Jimmy Choo sling back pumps while resting on Stiles' desk with both palms. "I am *not* going to do this with you, brother-in-law. Your brother is locked away just like you said for at least the next ten years if not the full twenty he was sentenced. He brought all this on himself. As for this church—New Holy Rock," she emphasized while looking around the large church office, "I will not step aside like a good little girl and let you take over my husband's ministry." Tapping her long, manicured nails on the desktop, she concentrated her stare on Stiles before briefly looking at Abel. "Abel can explain all the financials to you. Of course you can stay on as associate pastor, and on top of that, we'll make sure the remainder of your contract is still honored."

Stiles looked at the dwarf who eased down out of his seat and stood next to Rianna.

"She's right," Abel said. "I have the paperwork here." He looked to his side, reached down next to the chair, then pulled a briefcase up and placed it on top of Stiles' desk. Opening it, he removed a manila folder and inside pulled out a stack of papers. "Everything is explained here. I'll be glad to go over the terms with you to make sure you understand. This is a little different, I mean with this being a religious establishment and all, but you'll see that you will be well provided for."

Stiles folded both arms, shook his head, and smiled. "You think Hezekiah is going to fall for this? If you do, you're a bigger fool than I thought."

"Read the papers. When you're done, give me or Abel a call and we'll finalize everything. I want the reigns of this church turned over to me in the next forty-five days. Until then, you will continue to carry out the weekly church services."

"And who exactly do you have in mind for the senior pastor role in my brother's absence?" Stiles asked, trying to keep his growing fury under wraps and remain godly.

Rianna smiled, twirled around, and looked over her shoulder as she and Abel prepared to leave. "Who else, but uh, me, of course. God can use anybody, right? Well, I just volunteered for the job."

Abel opened the office door and allowed Rianna to strut out ahead of him.

Stiles watched from his office window as Rianna and her sidekick walked to her car.

Who did she think he was? Did she think she could just waltz her behind up in his office and demand he step aside and let her take over New Holy Rock. He turned from the window and walked back to his desk. His brother was right; Rianna was a force to be reckoned with, but the last thing Stiles wanted was for her to take over and destroy everything Hezekiah had worked hard for. No way was he going to let that happen.

†

Stiles made the bi-monthly five hour drive to Bledsoe Correctional Facility, also known as BCCX. The 2,500 acre prison was nestled in the hills between Pikeville and Spencer, Tennessee. His brother had been tucked away behind prison walls going on two years. He would visit with Hezekiah, catch him up on things happening in the ministry, and bring him up to date about family and life in general all while trying to keep his brother's spirits up. Some times were harder than others and Stiles could see why. Being locked up was something he didn't wish on his brother. Then again, Stiles understood that everyone has to pay for the consequences of their sins. Everyone reaps what they sow. Hezekiah was not a bad guy, but he did have some demons he was wrestling with. Demons Stiles prayed his brother would be delivered from while he was incarcerated. He didn't know how this latest round of news about Rianna was going to go. He could only pray that Hezekiah wouldn't go off into a tirade.

Upon arriving, Stiles studied the endless rows of thick barbed wire surrounding the prison. Stiles never got over how horrible it made him feel when he saw the complex. He mumbled a short prayer that the visit would go smoothly as he pulled into the VISITOR PARKING LOT.

After standing in a long snail moving line with other visitors, he was given a thorough search before he was allowed inside the complex where he found a round steel table with matching steel chairs. He sat down and waited.

Hezekiah came through the door after Stiles had been waiting for almost half an hour.

His brother looked freshly shaved and his dull gray prison garb looked like it had been in a dry cleaner with hardly a wrinkle.

"What's up, brother?" Hezekiah said, smiling big as he approached Stiles, gave him dap, and the two men sat across from each other.

"God is good."

"Yes, all the time," Hezekiah countered.

"You're looking good," Stiles complimented.

"Thanks. I won't complain."

The brothers exchanged general conversation until Stiles cleared his throat, gave his brother a sturdy look, almost frowning.

"What's on your mind? Please don't tell me that crazy woman I married is giving you trouble."

Stiles hesitated before speaking. "It's not that she's giving me trouble. It's that she wants to do some things I don't agree with and I know you won't agree with either. When was the last time she visited?"

"A month ago at least. Nothing's changed with her."

"She told me she was here a few days ago."

"A lie ain't nothing for her to tell," Hezekiah huffed. "Hah, my first lady is MIA, and when I call from the prison phone she refuses the calls. When I use my cell she ignores the call. I wouldn't be surprised if she has me BLOCKED. I don't know. Anyway, made up my mind, I'm going to divorce her. I'm not sitting up in here while she's out there spending my money and running up credit card debt in my name. I know I'm behind these bars, man, and ain't too much I can do but as long as I keep praising God and keep believing then I know He's going to deliver me from here soon, real soon."

Stiles nodded. "I agree with you on that."

"She might think she's getting away with screwing me over, but listen here, brother, there is not a friend or enemy who ever wronged Hezekiah McCoy that has not been repaid in full. You can bet on that," he boasted between a light cough.

"I hear you, but thing is she makes a good argument."

Clearing his throat and wiping his brow with the back of his hand, Hezekiah said, "What kind of good argument? Don't tell me she got to you." He laughed.

"I don't think you'll find it funny when I tell you her plans to take over New Holy Rock. She brought along some guy named Abel Cane with her. What a name. But besides that, she said he's her financial consultant." Stiles smirked.

"Is that right?" Hezekiah shook his head in bewilderment.

"She even went so far as demanding that I step aside from interim senior pastor and appoint her to serve in that capacity. I don't like to name call, but I'm beginning to think your first lady is a certified nut." Stiles shook his head while cautiously looking around at the roomful of other prisoners and visitors.

Hezekiah chuckled loudly, leaning back in the steel chair and flailing his arms like he was in disbelief. "One thing about Rianna."

"What's that?" Stiles looked at his brother curiously with a smile appearing on his lightly bearded face.

"There's never a dull moment with her," Hezekiah said, continuing to laugh until he started coughing.

"You okay?" Stiles asked, again.

"Yeah, I'm good. Sinuses or something, I think. Been doing a lot of it lately. Guess I'm allergic to this place," he said, chuckling lightly. "Tell me, what's up with the investigation into my shooting. Any new information?"

"Nah, I wish I had something to tell ya, but the case is cold as ice. After your partner George died, it's been hard to find someone we can trust to investigate it. Do you ever hear from the dude who used to be with y'all? I can't think of his name."

"You're probably talking about Benny."

"Yeah, I think that was his name."

"Nah, I haven't heard from him since George died. Last I heard he'd gotten himself in some kinda trouble and supposedly left town. I think I may have found someone who can do some looking out for me on the outside. One of the inmates who attends my Sunday service has a cousin that's supposed to be a private investigator. Says he might be able to get me hooked up with him. Of course, money talks. I don't know how much more of that I have. Not with my wife running around like she's married to Kanye or somebody."

Stiles grinned.

"Sounds good. We need someone who can look into it with a fresh set of eyes. You still don't remember anything else about that evening?"

"Other than the voice sounded sort of familiar. Then again, I remember it sounded like he was talking through something, like those singers who do auto tune. I don't know much else."

"We won't give up until we find out who it was that tried to take you out."

"I can't sit behind these bars for too much longer," Hezekiah said, suddenly showing signs of frustration and irritability.

"You're going to get out of here. And it's not going to take twenty years."

"I want to believe that, but the judge denied the attorney's previous request to release me on parole."

"And what was the reason for that? I forget."

"I refused to participate in a treatment program for sex offenders and violence prevention. Hell, why would I participate in something like that when I'm not a sex offender," Hezekiah almost shouted.

"Yeah, but that was just one upset. We're going to tackle every obstacle and you watch, we're going to win. Your lawyer has already filed two challenges with the Tennessee Supreme Court. Have you heard anything from that?" Stiles asked.

"No, only that he believes I stand a good chance of them releasing me. They're arguing that the judge's decision to let prosecutors call those other accusers tainted my trial. The other issue raised was that I had a prior agreement with the former prosecutor that I'd never be charged."

"We're going to stay in prayer and remain faithful. Remember, God's plans for you are not to harm you, my brother, but to give you hope and a future. And that future is not going to be spent behind these prison bars."

"I agree." Hezekiah started coughing again.

"You sure you okay? I know I'm laying a lot on you, but I try to get in as much as I can since I don't come up here but every couple months. Trying to tell you what's going on over the phone isn't the same."

"Tell me about it. I have to watch my words when I call from these prison phones. And every time I use my cell, I'm taking a chance of being caught with illegal contraband. But it's all good. Now that I've gotten that settled, tell me how's my son? Let me rephrase that. How are my sons and grandkids?"

"They're good. I have some new pictures in my phone of the grandkids I took especially for you." Stiles retrieved his cell phone out of his pocket and began showing Hezekiah pictures of his grandchildren.

Tears formed in his eyes. He swiftly swiped them away with his hand. "They're beautiful, and the boys have gotten so big. And look at this little cutie," he pointed at the image of Khaliyah, "they were *soooo* certain she was going to be a boy." Hezekiah started laughing again. "God definitely has a sense of humor."

"Yeah, he does," agreed Stiles.

"And what about you? You got any prospects? I know some of those ladies are joining New Holy Rock because there's a half way good looking single pastor behind the pulpit." He laughed.

"Half way good looking? Naw, you didn't go there."

"Admit it, you can't be as good looking as me, my brother." Hezekiah laughed again but his laughter turned into a coughing spell again, only this time it was more aggressive. Sweat beads popped out on his brow.

Stiles looked around and made eye contact with one of the correction officers when Hezekiah's cough caused him to start choking and gasping for air, clenching one hand around his throat.

A tall white blonde haired CO with sagging uniform pants walked swiftly over and tried to see if he could help provide Hezekiah some relief. When Hezekiah passed out, and his head slammed against the table top, it was obvious he needed medical attention.

Stiles was standing over him, next to the CO, and tried lifting Hezekiah's head off the table. "Call somebody! Anybody! He's gone unconscious," Stiles said to a shocked looking guard.

"Help, I need to get him to the infirmary. Quick!" a female guard said to one of the other officers who in turn ran to the front of the visitor area where other correction officers were stationed behind a glass partition.

Stiles watched, his eyes going from his unconscious brother and what was going on at the front. Minutes later, two "Terminator" sized guards arrived. They placed the weight of Hezekiah under each of their arms and dragged him out of the area.

"Where are you taking him?" Stiles asked, his voice unsteady.

"To the infirmary. You can leave your contact information at the front desk. Someone will be in touch," one of the guards said.

Stiles watched until they disappeared behind steel plated doors before he turned and raced to the front office to leave his information.

two

"Cheating is easy; try something more challenging like being faithful." Unknown

Rianna stood on the balcony of her luxurious hotel suite with a spectacular view of the Seattle waterfront, her fresh newly purchased lace front flowing in the wind. Big Daddy had come home for a few days to visit his wife and to tend to some business affairs. He invited Rianna to join him. The first class flight from Memphis to Seattle was more than she had bargained for. She felt special, like a real live celebrity! This was exactly how she imagined her life should be.

The day after arriving, she got a call from the prison informing her that her husband had a heart attack.

"Is he....is he alive?" she asked, placing a hand over her chest.

"Yes, he's stable. He's expected to survive, but we transferred him to Bledsoe Hospital until he's out of the woods. We'll notify you when we have more information. Will you be coming?"

"Uhh, no, I'm not in Tennessee right now. But please, call me if there's any change."

"Sure," the man on the other end said, sounding unenthusiastic.

"Thank you," Rianna said and ended the call. "Hey, Tiny," Rianna said when she called and Tiny picked up on the third ring.

"Hey, girl. Where you at?" Tiny sounded like she had a wad of gum or food in her mouth as she spoke.

"You won't believe it when I tell you. I'm in Seattle, girl."

"Seattle? Seattle what?"

"Seattle, Washington, fool."

"Are you serious?"

"Yep, I flew here. First class...with Big Daddy. He came up here to see his wife and handle some business. He asked if I wanted to tag along. You know I was not about to turn down a free trip. It's so beautiful here, Tiny. I've never seen anything like it. It's a little rainy today but still it's breathtaking. Girl, I feel like Michelle Obama."

"You get all the breaks. You're making me jealous," Tiny said, giggling.

"No worries, we're still going on our girl's trip this summer. I don't know where, but we're going to run up Hezekiah's black card and have ourselves a ball. Heck, we may even come up here."

"Ohhhh, I can't wait," Tiny giggled some more. "So what are you doing while Big Daddy is playing the faithful husband?"

"I'm at the hotel right now, standing out on a beautiful balcony overlooking the Seattle waterfront. Later I'm going out to see what this city has to offer. Big Daddy left me with a wad of cash so you already know I'm going to spend every cent."

"You betta. After all, you only live once."

"I know that's right. Oh, before I forget, I just got a call from the prison. Hezekiah had a heart attack, girl. Can you believe that?"

"What? A heart attack? Is he? Is he alive?" Tiny asked, pausing between each word.

"Yeah," Rianna said, nonchalantly. "He's still in the land of the living. That fool has more lives than a cat. I'll be back home the first of the week. When I get back I plan to drive up there to see what's going on. They transferred him to Bledsoe Hospital, I think, that's the name of it. It's close to the prison. The social worker is supposed to call me when they hear anything more about his condition, but they expect him to pull through."

"Girl, you're right, that man definitely has nine lives. He's had a stroke, been shot, and now he's had a heart attack. I guess God ain't through with him yet," Tiny offered.

"Or the devil," added Rianna and the besties burst into laughter.

†

Five days after visiting Hezekiah, Stiles still hadn't heard a word from the prison social worker or the infirmary about his brother's condition. He had tried calling Rianna several times but got no answer from her either. He followed up with several text messages. Three days later she texted him back.

"Out of town. Have news about Hezekiah. Will call when I get back in a few days."

Stiles called the prison several times a day. Each time he got the run around, was put on an extended hold, or given conflicting information. Today's phone call sent him into a fury.

"Sorry, sir, they should have told you. We can only give information about an inmate to his next of kin," the rude sounding woman said on the other end.

"I *am* his next of kin. I'm his brother," Stiles explained, trying to maintain his composure so the woman wouldn't detect his growing frustration. "My name should be on the visitation list—Stiles Graham."

The woman didn't respond for several seconds. "I see a uhh, Reverend Stiles Graham. Is that you?"

"Yes. That's me. Now please tell me about my brother," he insisted.

"Like I said, we can only give information on inmates to the next of kin. It says here that you're his... pastor." She paused. "Oh, wait, I see they have you down as his brother too. But I still can't give you any information. The next of kin is listed as his wife. And uh, looks like she's designated that she be the only one we give personal inmate information to. I suggest you get in touch with her. She should be able to tell you about the inmate's condition."

"But—"

A dial tone sounded in Stiles' ear. "Dang it!" he mouthed and pressed END on his phone. He was getting ready to call Rianna again when his cell phone rang. It was Fancy.

"Have you heard anything?" a concerned Fancy asked. She was absolutely beside herself with worry when Stiles called and told her Hezekiah had fallen ill. She shot off one question after another. "Rianna hasn't called you back yet? What about the prison social worker? Is there anyone else you can call?"

"Nobody," he said, frustration ringing in his voice. "I hope whatever made him pass out was not something serious. And I hate to say it, but

Rianna's lack of interest in her husband's well-being reveals that woman is ruthless. She acts like she has no real concern or love for my brother."

"I can't believe you're just realizing that. Rianna Jamison is no good but I can't say Hezekiah doesn't deserve some of what he's getting. I mean, you and I know, although we love him, he's not exactly an angel. He may be a man of God, but sometimes he acts like he's ruled by the devil. I know I shouldn't say things like that about him, but it is what it is. Maybe while he's in prison, he'll change. I mean starting up that Sunday service while he's in there was a good start. It's just that I don't know if he's sincere about that. But that's between him and the good Lord."

"I think he's sincere. If you talked to him like I do, then you would see there's a change in him. I mean, it's subtle, but I still detect it. This last visit he seemed different. I think the Lord is dealing with him behind those prison walls. I think whenever he gets released he's going to be a better man."

"I hope so, but I also pray that he won't be away for twenty years either. He'll be seventy-one years old! Okay, so he's done his share of wrong, but deep down inside I know he loves God. He's just caught up in the ways of this world like a lot of Christian folks are. I pray for him every single day," Fancy lamented.

"Fancy, wait....hol' up. Let me call you back. This is Rianna calling."

"Okay, call me back."

Stiles quickly clicked over to the incoming call.

"Uh, I just called to let you know that I'm taking over New Holy Rock, effective immediately. No ifs, ands or buts about it. Not only is Hezekiah incarcerated, he had a heart attack."

"What? A heart attack? I didn't think it was that serious." Stiles declared, alarmed to hear his brother had suffered such a serious illness. He thought perhaps Hezekiah had gotten dehydrated or maybe he had the flu or covid, but a heart attack was not even his mind.

"Oh, please, don't get your nuts in a wad; he's not dead; he's in stable condition. The doctor said he expects him to pull through but they transferred him to a hospital near the prison. He'll be there for a few days and then they'll transfer him back to the prison infirmary, his cell, or whatever," she said nonchalantly. "Anyway, just so you know, I'm bringing in a guest preacher to deliver the message next Sunday."

"Not now, Rianna. You must have lost your mind. I don't see how can you be thinking about some guest preacher when my brother just had a heart attack. You're one evil..." Stiles retorted. It took a lot to set him off or make him display his anger. This was one of those times. Before he knew it, he had called Rianna the *B* word. "I'm sorry, I didn't mean that," he immediately apologized.

Rianna laughed into the phone, sounding like a cackling evil witch. "My, my, my. Whaddaya know, my brotha-n-law actually has a backbone. I find it sorta cute. Anyway, talk to you later, brotha-n-law. I have things to do and folks to see." Rianna ended the call without waiting on Stiles to reply.

Moments later, Abel appeared. "How'd he take hearing the news you're bringing in a guest pastor?" Abel asked, standing in Rianna's bedroom door shirtless with his taunt abs on display and wearing fitted tiny black boxer briefs.

Rianna displayed a wicked grin after ending the call with Stiles. She sauntered over to where Big Daddy stood. "What could he say? To me, it went perfect, absolutely perfect. And what makes it even easier is that I just found out my ol' man had a heart attack. And before you get your hopes up, he's not dead. The prison said he was transferred to a nearby hospital. I told them I was out of town but when I returned I would drive up and check on him. They're supposed to call me if anything changes." She got down on her knees, making herself eye level with Big Daddy, and placed a deep kiss on his lips. "Let's celebrate," she cooed. "Oh," she said, rising to her feet as Big Daddy went toward the bed, "remember we need to find a guest preacher for Sunday service."

†

Stiles got up from his sofa, went into the kitchen, and retrieved a cold beer, guzzling it down. Slamming his balled fist on the white and grey quartz countertop, he shook his head, bit down on his bottom lip, and stormed out of the kitchen.

He called Fancy back and told her the dreadful news. She was relieved to know Hezekiah was going to recover, but she was still highly upset that she and Stiles had no access to him. She wanted to see him for herself, but she was not on his visitor's list, thanks to Rianna. She rarely heard from Hezekiah and when she did the conversations were less than a couple of minutes. It was no time to say hardly anything but how are you and take care of yourself.

"Can't you go see him as his pastor?" Fancy asked.

"No, not until he's been cleared to receive visitors again."

She hated that, but there was nothing she could do about it. Hezekiah didn't want to cause confusion in his marriage, especially with Rianna being the one who had the power to call all the shots. What on God's green earth could that man have been thinking to give someone like Rianna access to his money?

She learned from Xavier that Hezekiah had added Rianna to one of his checking accounts and on top of that his ongoing salary from New Holy Rock was being paid directly to her. She never did right by him but Fancy was not surprised.

Fancy didn't chastise him the few times he had called. It was bad enough that he was sitting in a cell doing time. She was all too familiar with how miserable that could be. She didn't wish that on anybody. Plus, this time she didn't think Hezekiah deserved to be locked up, surely not for twenty years. She still believed it had been a set up by someone, only God knows who, to pin those sexual charges with a minor on him. It had unfortunately worked and now Hezekiah was behind bars...again.

"Have you heard from him lately?" Stiles asked.

"No, and it's better this way. I respect the fact he's married, plus I'm extra cautious. I don't want to get tangled up with him again. Ex-husband or not, I'm not about to get involved with someone else's husband. I don't care if it *is* somebody like Rianna. He's married and I respect that."

"You're a good woman, Fancy," Stiles complimented. "My brother screwed up when he lost you."

"Things happen for a reason, Stiles. I loved Hezekiah, but I didn't or I should say I couldn't keep putting up with his ways. He was a cheater and a liar. He even had a kid while we were married," Fancy said, tears forming. "I know God can change anybody, and one day maybe he will change Hezekiah, but I can't worry about that. I have to keep my walk with God as straight as possible. Then again, I won't sit back and let Rianna or anyone get away with walking all over him, especially while he's not out here to defend himself."

"Well, Rianna better tread carefully because payback ain't no joke. She's digging some pretty deep ditches for herself. Oh, and guess what else she's come up with. You're going to fall out laughing when you hear this," Stiles said, laughing himself.

"What?"

"She's inviting a guest preacher to deliver the message next Sunday."

"What did you say?"

"You heard me. She says she's taking over New Holy Rock. She wants to be the senior pastor in Hezekiah's absence, but until she takes on that role, she said she's bringing in guest speakers. I didn't even have the energy to argue with her. God has to handle her."

Fancy's tears turned to laughter. "You have got to be kidding."

"I wish I was but you know I'm not."

"Well, I wouldn't miss this for all the tea in China. If it's the good Lord's will, I'm going to be there Sunday. I want to see who this so called guest preacher is going to be," Fancy said.

"You and me both. You think Xavier knows what's going on?"

"What do you mean? I told him *and* Khalil their father had fallen ill. I still need to call and let them know it was a heart attack," Fancy said, worry resonating in her weak voice. "God, please heal him," she mouthed.

"Okay, do that. But we know Hezekiah's going to be fine. God's got him," Stiles assured. "As for Xavier, I haven't said anything to him yet about Rianna's plans. I've been busy and before I put that on his shoulders, I thought I'd talk to the trustees and deacons first. But I do need to talk to him soon. Hezekiah wants me to look into removing her name as the payee for his church salary."

"That's a smart move on his part. Well, look, I'm going to fix myself a sandwich. I missed dinner. Thanks for calling me back. While I'm eating I'm going to call Xavier and Khalil and tell them the latest news about their father. Call me if you hear anything else. I don't care what time of day or night. Oh, and I don't think we should tell Pastor and Josie. At least not yet. Plus, Pastor may or may not remember Hezekiah anyway."

"Yeah, I don't think he will. He has a hard time recognizing *me* some days," Stiles said somberly. "Alzheimer's is such a terrible disease."

"Yeah, it is, but God is able."

"Amen," said Stiles. "Well, go ahead and call Xavier and Khalil. We'll talk tomorrow. Good night."

"Goodnight, Stiles, and thanks again."

three

"Secrets are festering parasites to a relationship, devouring their hosts from within, leaving behind an empty hollow husk of what once was." Mark Boyer

Most Wednesday nights after weekly Bible study Khalil's normal routine was to sleep over at Detria's home. However, since Eliana had given birth to his daughter, he had all but gone ghost. It had been weeks since he'd been in Detria's bed or even stopped by her house. She tried enticing him, telling him she had his favorite smoke but Khalil turned her down every time.

"Look," she remembered him telling her the last time he went over there, which was a few days after Eliana gave birth, *"I can't do this anymore. I have a kid now. I can't be coming over here laying up with you when I have a daughter and wife at home who need me. We both know what this was and that it wasn't gonna last forever."*

Tonight she'd had enough. No way was she going to let Khalil just exit out of her life like what they'd shared the past four years had meant nothing. She knew he cared about her; she didn't care what he said. If it wasn't for Eliana and that dang baby he would still be sharing her bed. Detria had to do something to get him back. This was just a phase he was going through. He was just excited because this was his first kid. Yeah, the more she thought about it, the more she told herself that he would come back to her bed.

News had gotten around Holy Rock that Hezekiah had a stroke or heart attack or something in prison. Detria didn't feel any type of way about it; but she thought she could find a way to use it to her advantage. How? She hadn't figured that much out, but somehow she had to get next to Khalil.

She dialed his phone number and it went to voicemail. She repeated calling him several times, each time her anger rising when he didn't answer.

Priscilla appeared in the kitchen where Detria was pacing nervously.

"How are you this afternoon? You've been pacing around here all day like a nervous cat. What's got you so aggravated?"

"Priscilla, I know you noticed that Khalil hasn't been over here in weeks."

"Yes, but things are different now, honey. The man has a child, not to mention a wife. I mean, seriously, you can't expect him to come over as much as before. Having a baby, especially a newborn, can be stressful. It takes a lot of adjusting to. Especially being it's their first child."

Detria threw up a hand, frustrated. "I don't care about him having a kid. He didn't give birth; his wife did. Anyway, I miss him, Priscilla. But he says we can't see each other like we did before ever since that little brat came into the world. I don't know what to do. Even at church, I can't get close to him for those dang armor bearers. Now he won't answer my calls or texts."

Priscilla glared at her, shaking her head while saying a prayer in her spirit for Detria who had become more like a surrogate daughter than her employer. She'd been working for Detria since Detria's accident and the two women had grown extremely close. She hated to see Detria troubled, especially over someone else's husband. But this was Detria's trademark. She was always hooking up with someone else's man.

"You deserve a man of your own, Detria, not someone else's man. I keep telling you that. I wish you would see yourself the way I see you, the way God sees you. You're beautiful, smart, and full of love. You are an amazing woman." Priscilla walked up to her and hugged her.

Detria accepted the show of affection and laid her head against Priscilla's shoulder. Tears flowed down her cheeks, landing on Priscilla's crisp white cotton uniform shirt.

"*Shhh,* it's going to be okay," Priscilla soothed her. "I've got you. You just have to learn how to let things be, Dee. All you need to do is let God have his way, sweet child. He wants you to be happy and whole."

Priscilla's words made Detria cry that much harder. It was if a dam had burst and tears flowed heavily until Detria was sobbing.

"Let it out," Priscilla urged. "Let it all out."

†

While Detria was at home crying her heart out, Khalil hurried home after midweek service to his wife and ten-month old daughter, Khaliyah. He rushed to park his car inside the garage and almost took off running after getting out of the car and going inside the house.

"*Helloooo,* Daddy's home," he said proudly, taking off upstairs when he didn't see Eliana or his little girl.

He bounded up the stairs two at a time until he arrived at the door to his daughter's room. He saw Eliana sitting in the rocking chair cradling a sleeping Khaliyah in her arms.

He pulled out his phone and took a couple of pictures of the two most important girls in his life.

Ambling over to them, he leaned in and kissed Eliana lightly on the top of her head.

Eliana stirred, opened her eyes, and looked up into Khalil's smiling face. She released a smile of her own.

"Hey, there," she whispered.

"Hey, sleepy head. You've had a tough day, huh?"

"No, it was good. Our daughter is the perfect little angel." Eliana kissed the sleeping baby and Khalil eased her out of Eliana's arms.

Khaliyah didn't wake up. Instead she nestled closer to her daddy's chest. Khalil walked around the room lightly shaking her while singing to her and planting butterfly kisses on her.

"You're going to wake her," Eliana said softly.

"It's okay. If she wakes up, I'll put her back to sleep."

"Good, it's your night to get up with her anyway."

"Yeah, I know. Why don't you go take one of those bubble baths you like or do whatever. Get you some rest. I've got our daughter." He walked back over to where Eliana was rising from the chair. The two of them kissed before Eliana disappeared out of the room.

Sticking her head back in the door briefly, she said, "Your dinner plate is in the microwave. All you need to do is heat it up. Dessert's in the fridge."

"Okay, gotcha."

This was the life Khalil was still getting accustomed to. He loved his daughter and Eliana was a good person and a great mother. He would be thirty years old in a couple of years. Never would he have imagined himself as the leader of a mega church with a wife and a beautiful daughter. He smiled when he remembered the ultrasound visit and the doctor told him and Eliana there they were having a boy, but God had other plans. Khalil smiled even bigger while looking down on Khaliyah. She was no bouncing baby boy but a precious beautiful little girl. He was beyond ecstatic. She was perfect.

He sat down in the chair cradling his daughter, and thinking about how far God had allowed him to come. From a troubled teen in and out of detention centers to where he was today. He was blessed and he knew he was. In spite of all the things he'd done that were not pleasing to God, God was still showing him favor. It was time to stop all the foolery and get his life on track. That was one thing he agreed with his friend Omar about. Removing Detria from his life was part of that plan, but that was proving to be harder than he expected. No matter what he told her or how he tried to explain that things were over between them, Detria wouldn't go away. She was always somewhere lurking, somewhere devising a plan to break up his marriage. He couldn't let that keep happening. He would do whatever he had to do to keep her from destroying what he was building.

"Obviously she still doesn't know who she's messing with, Khaliyah," he whispered to the sleeping baby. "But if she keeps stirring the pot she's going to find out what's cooking—Daddy can promise you that."

four

"Never let a problem that needs to be solved take precedence over a person who needs to be loved." Unknown

Khalil and Xavier dined on overfilled plates of soul food at one of the Mom and Pop neighborhood restaurants a few miles from New Holy Rock. Khalil had surprisingly contacted his younger brother and inquired about doing a walk through of New Holy Rock, something he had been planning to do for months after the religious facility opened its doors, but hadn't—until today.

"The church looks good. Y'all have been doing it up over there, huh?" remarked Khalil.

"You know Pops wouldn't have it any other way. Everything has to be the best and finest from the church pews, to the pulpit, to the carpeted floors. Everything."

"Yeah, that's him," agreed Khalil. "Any word about his condition since the heart attack?"

"No, not really. All I know is he's expected to recover. Stiles has been trying to reach Rianna. Last time me and him spoke, she hadn't returned any of his calls or texts."

"Praise God he's going to be okay. I mean you have to admit, he's had his share of crises. First the stroke, then he was shot, and now the heart attack. I'm glad he's going to be okay and that it didn't take him out, but you and I both know what goes around comes around."

"I know you aren't implying that he deserved to have a heart attack?"

"Nah, I'm just saying hopefully this will be a wakeup call for him. He's been doing some wild and crazy stuff for as long as I can remember. Some of it, you have to admit he's paying for. I mean, you're talking about an already fifty-year old man looking at spending twenty years of his life in prison, and having a heart attack or getting any illness in prison is not exactly the best thing that can happen to him or anyone. No telling what kind of medical treatment he's getting."

"I don't know much about the hospital where they sent him. They won't let family other than Rianna visit him. When was the last time you saw him?

"I haven't seen him since they locked him up. I'm not on his visitor's log. It's not like we were exactly best buds before he got locked up. I mean, you know what time it is."

"I do, but sometimes you have to be the bigger person. I'm not telling you that you have to forget all the grievances the two of you have.

I know you just like I know Pops. Both of you are hotheaded. I don't know if you took that money from him and I don't care. What I do know is it's time to let bygones be bygones. You're growing in the ministry. You have a beautiful family. A precious little girl. And with this latest brush of death with our dad, don't you think it's time you show some forgiveness?"

Khalil took a forkful of his thick juicy roast before answering his brother. "You're right. I won't argue with you on that. But I don't think we'll ever be as close as you and him. And then when I found out he had cheated on Ma and he has another kid out there. I mean, come on, Xavier, the man is wildin' out. Ma didn't deserve that."

"Ma is good. She's a strong woman. Plus, you and I both know this isn't the first time Ma and Dad have had problems in their marriage. But that's all behind her now. They're divorced and she's free to go on with her life. Sure, he's done some awful things and he hasn't always treated her the way she deserves to be treated, but you can't deny that she loves the man. I believe he still loves her too. That may sound a little crazy but it is what it is."

"You think Dad really did what he was accused of with underage girls?" Khalil asked, taking a swallow of his ice water to wash down the remnants of his roast.

"I don't believe he did. But if he did, he wasn't aware that the girl was underage. He's done some shady stuff but I don't think he's a child molester or whatever. His lawyer is trying to get him off on some technicality, but I don't know how that's gonna work," Xavier remarked. This time it was Xavier who took several bites of his fried chicken, followed by a forkful of his macaroni and cheese, and then a forkful of turnip greens.

"Speaking of these females out there," Xavier said, swallowing his mouthful of food, "what's up with you and Detria? Please tell me you're done with her. I thought it would be enough for you when you found out she had slept with Dad, and then she was married to Uncle Stiles, had a baby with his best friend, and you still smashing that? I don't get it. I never have," cautioned Xavier.

"That was a smash and grab. Plus, ol' girl took good care of me. But to answer your question, I cut that off. I can't deny that I do sorta miss her. I mean she kept me with plenty of green and whatever a dude wanted."

"I thought you had stopped smoking that stuff when you got married," Xavier questioned.

"I did, but I'm just saying Detria gives me whatever I want. But I can't keep playing out here. Too much is going on. With that pandemic stuff and folks going bat crazy in these streets, I need to stay close to the crib. I'm not trying to bring trouble to my home or to Holy Rock. And, you know, it's funny you should mention Detria, because I was telling God that I need to do some things different in my life, you know. I realize how blessed I am. I don't want to screw that up like my Pops did with Ma and us."

"I'm glad to hear you say that. I think Eliana's a good girl. She seems to love you and now that y'all have that beautiful niece of mine, I know you don't want to do anything to jeopardize your family."

"Straight up,"

"Okay, sop enough about me and Eliana. What's up with you and Pepper?"

Xavier paused, swallowed a few times and then briefly looked at his brother before looking back down at his plate.

"Uh, I take it that things aren't going like you hoped. You look like you saw a ghost when I mentioned Pepper."

"I guess it's going okay. She's a good mother and she tries to be a good wife, but....man I don't know, Khalil. I'm just not feeling her, the marriage, or the whole happy family thing. I like her. I mean I might even love her if that makes sense. But I can't say that I'm *in* love with her. Know what I mean?"

"Most definitely," said Khalil. "I feel you."

Xavier stopped picking at his food and looked at his brother. "What do you mean? Aren't you in love with Eliana?"

"Like you, I love her, but as for being *in* love, I don't think so. But that doesn't mean that I'm not going to do whatever I can to make my marriage work now that I have a daughter. I think you should do the same. You have two boys and they need their father. You and I both know how important that is. We grew up having both parents in the household, no matter how many bad times they may have experienced. I want that for my daughter. I don't want to miss one moment with her."

"Yeah, I feel the same, but as for my personal life, I can't say I'm happy or if I'll ever be happy. Uh, I know you don't like me to talk about him with you, but has Eliana said anything about Ian?"

Khalil looked at his brother like he was surprised at the question. "You don't know?"

"Know what?" said Xavier, puzzled.

"Ian moved to the ATL a few weeks ago. He got a job at one of the schools down there. Eliana said he met some dude online and off he went," Khalil said, smiling and then he turned serious again. “I think you need to let that part of your life go and concentrate on being a good dad and an even better husband. One thing I can say about Pepper is she accepts you just the way you are. She’s never looked at you differently because you’re gay. I don’t know how she does it, but hey it works for her so who am I to judge. She’s one of those women who believes the power of her sex is better than what any same sex relationship can do for you.” Khalil briefly smiled and took another bite of food.

“Yeah, she thinks I’m supposed to be able to turn my desires on and off like a light switch, but it’s hard. And again,” Xavier reiterated, “I know you don’t like to hear me talk about my sexuality but then again you’re my brother. I need to be able to talk to somebody. I’d rather talk to you than some therapist or shady so-called friends.” Xavier shook his head and looked around the restaurant like he was expecting someone to give him a dirty look. No one seemed to be paying attention to the brothers so Xavier continued.

“I had no idea Ian had left Memphis. I haven’t heard from him since we parted ways, and whenever I see your wife, she doesn’t or won’t say much. I guess it makes her uncomfortable too. But she knows how I feel about Ian. Maybe she thinks if she doesn’t say anything that it's like what me and him had never happened." Xavier's eyes watered but he held back his tears.

"This food is delicious. It's only the second time I've been here," said Khalil, changing the subject, hoping it would keep his brother from crying like a woman. He couldn't tolerate that. It was bad enough that he had to sit and listen to his brother talking about his heartbreak over some dude, but if he started crying Khalil already knew he would have to get up and leave.

Hearing that Ian had moved away without bothering to let him know hit Xavier like a ton of bricks. But maybe this was for the best. Maybe Ian moving out of town would force Xavier to accept that part of his life was indeed over. He had to focus on his family like his brother suggested, but how would he be able to stay married to Pepper for years to come? Would he be able to let his past stay in the past? He couldn't promise that. Looking up and to his right, his eyes connected with a handsome Asian man at a table near where he and Khalil sat. The man was sitting across the table from another equally handsome man but Xavier's eyes settled on the handsomely dressed Asian sporting a thin mustache, black straight hair and a smile to die for. Xavier quickly looked away. "Lord, help me," he whispered.

"Hey, you good?" Khalil asked, following his brother's eyes and seeing the men sitting at the other table.

"Oh, yea, I'm straight," Xavier answered, taking another quick glance at the handsome stranger.

"Don't even think about it," Khalil advised.

"I can't promise I won't think about it, but I can promise you that I won't act on my feelings. Like you said, I have a wife and kids. I'm going to give them my all."

"Now that's the brother I'm talking about," Khalil said and smiled. "What do you say we get out of here and go to my crib and shoot some pool. The game is coming on later. We can watch that too."

"Nah, I can't. Not tonight anyway." Xavier looked at his watch. "I need to get out of here. I have to go back to New Holy Rock and finish up some paperwork before I head to the house. Pepper is going to get her hair braided. I told her I would be there in time to watch the boys. She wants a part-time nanny. What do you think about that?"

"I think it's a good idea. These moms today aren't built like mothers of yesterday. They need all the help they can get, so if hiring help is something you want to do and it's financially straight for you, then I say go for it. Plus, Pepper has had a rough time these past couple of years." Khalil picked up his napkin and wiped his mouth. The server approached. "May we have our checks please?"

"Yes sir," the server said and walked away.

"Yeah, you're right, the boys can definitely be a handful. There's always something they're into and Pepper still has moments when I question her mental health. Since she didn't go back to work after giving birth it's like she never has a break from them. I don't want to set her off or do anything that might disturb her mentally. She's been doing really well ever since she came back home, but there are still times when I see her frustration and how the boys can work her nerves. It's not often, but if she says she needs help, then you know I want to give her what she needs."

"And you should. No doubt. She fought to regain her sanity and her health. That's a good thing. Thank God for healing," said Khalil.

Moments later, after paying their checks, the brothers left out the restaurant and walked toward their cars parked next to each other.

They gave each other a hug. "Talk to you later. Let's get together more often," suggested Khalil. "After all, we *are* brothers," he said, laughing.

"You're right. Let's make it happen," said Xavier, also chuckling before getting in his car.

"Bet. Oh, and remember to let me know when you hear something about Dad."

five

"The greater the power, the more dangerous the abuse." Edmund Burke

After the late afternoon lunch with Khalil, Xavier returned to New Holy Rock to finish up some administrative paperwork before he set out for home. He pondered over the things he and his brother talked about. Particularly, the part about making their marriages work and letting go of the past.

His mind reflected on his life and lifestyle. From his first homosexual encounter with Raymone to his relationship with Ian, suddenly he felt strange, out of place, like he was having what he could only describe as an out of body experience. His thoughts raced through his mind as he relived both relationships and how they had affected his life and life's decisions. What had happened to his longtime desire to attend college, go away to Xavier University and start a whole new life? That had all but gone down the drain. Sure, he took online college courses and right before the start of the pandemic in 2020, he received his Bachelor's degree in Finance. It didn't completely fulfill him because he had other dreams he once desired. Hooking up with Pepper and running off marrying her had been the start of his demise. Or was it? Perhaps his life had started spiraling out of control after the terrible car accident involving Raymone. Whatever it was, or whenever it started, all Xavier knew was he wasn't happy in his marriage or with his life. Yet he was stuck, at least that's what he took from the conversation with his brother, although neither said those exact words.

At his office he finished downloading some financial documents, replied to a few emails, including one from Stiles about his father's inquiry into paying his attorney fees, and then he set out for home. The good thing about going home was the excitement he felt about seeing his sons. They were his one true blessing that he thanked God for every single day.

As he passed by the church sanctuary going toward the EXIT sign, he stopped, stood at the entrance, and then slowly walked inside the quiet, peaceful space. He silently ambled toward the altar, almost as if he was on auto pilot. Standing before the altar, he began to pray for his father, asking God to heal Hezekiah and bring him out of the hospital whole and to restore his father's health. He thanked God for his family, his mom, his kids, and his wife. Lastly, with tears now pouring from his eyes, Xavier prayed for himself.

"God, help me to fight against the war raging with my fleshly desires. Keep me truthful and faithful to my wife and family. Help me not succumb to the desires of my flesh and to desire only my wife. I don't want to feel this way but you know how hard I find living this lifestyle, Father God." He recalled a scripture he had heard often in his life. It fit the situation he found himself in. "I know your Word tells us temptation comes from our own desires, which entice us and drag us away," he prayed. "God, this is why I can't do this without you. Thank you for keeping me."

Xavier wiped his tears and turned away. Leaving out of the sanctuary, he walked outside the church where he was met with a rainy mist. The bushes lining the well landscaped church grounds gently swayed with the flow of the wind as the drops of rain fell. The warmth from earlier in the day was turning to a refreshing coolness.

Xavier paused on the church steps before going to his personal parking space. Sitting inside his vehicle, he eyed an incoming text message from Trevor Price, the attorney who had handled his now *off the table* divorce.

"Received some surprising information about your father. call when you get this message. TP"

What did Trevor have to tell him?"

He continued the drive home, deciding to wait until he got there before calling Trevor. No texting and driving for him. He'd had his share of horrific accidents. He turned up the volume on the radio and started singing along with Kirk Franklin...*"I don't wanna love nobody but you..."*

Nineteen minutes later he turned into his driveway. He remained in his car, blindly watching the gentle stream of rain against his windshield. He inhaled the refreshing scent with eyes closed before opening them and calling Trevor.

Trevor's voicemail popped on after several rings.

"Hey, Trevor, it's Xavier...uh Xavier McCoy returning your call. I have to admit, man, you have my curiosity piqued. Can't imagine what's going on. Hit me back."

Xavier pressed the overhead garage door remote inside his vehicle and drove toward the door as it opened.

Inside the house, he was welcomed by the aroma of food. He entered the kitchen situated to the right and off the interior garage door entrance. Stepping further into the kitchen and moving around the large rectangular quartz topped island, he ventured toward the stove. Each pot he opened had something delicious in it. Pasta, baked barbeque chicken, green beans, fried corn, and a skillet of cornbread. Pepper could cook her behind off. Xavier understood why she needed a part-time nanny. No way could she take care of two rambunctious boys, run the household, take time for herself, and prepare a meal such as this at least three to four days a week. He admired her for putting forth more than a hundred percent effort into their marriage and motherhood. This made him more determined to do the same.

Pepper, seemingly unheard by Xavier, sauntered up behind him and wrapped her arms around his waist.

Xavier turned around, returned her embrace, and kissed her deeply.

"The boys are down for the night. They played so hard they tired themselves out," she whispered between his kisses.

With no further words, she took him by his hand and led him to their bedroom.

Xavier inhaled, slowly exhaled. *You got this.* He took the lead and romantically led his wife the remainder of the way.

Pepper gloried in his assertiveness revealed in her wide smile. *Thank you, God.*

†

Khalil made a pit stop at Detria's house before heading home. He had to end things officially once and for all—AGAIN.

He rang Detria's doorbell. Priscilla answered. Her furrowed brows couldn't hide the scowl on her face when she saw him. She seemed to try to quickly change her expression and greeted him cordially.

"Hello, Pastor McCoy," she said, clearing her throat. "Come in." She stepped aside. Turning around, she called, "Detria...Detria," she repeated as Khalil proceeded into the house.

Detria appeared, almost running down the stairs when she saw Khalil. "Khalil, baby, what a surprise. I didn't know you were coming."

Priscilla rolled her eyes, but out of view from Detria and disappeared down the long hallway.

"Yeah, I'm sorry about that. We need to talk, Dee."

"No need to apologize. Mi casa is still your casa," she said, giggling.

"I'm serious, Detria." He looked to his left as if looking for Priscilla. Seemingly satisfied that she'd left out of the area, he walked toward Detria as she took the last step down the stairs.

She grabbed hold of his hand and stood on her tiptoes and kissed him.

Khalil turned his face and the kiss landed on his cheek. Stepping back, he abruptly took hold of Detria's hand. "It's not that kinda party." He forcefully guided her into the family room.

"What's wrong?" Detria asked, agitated.

"Look, you've got to stop. I've told you before, Dee, stop blowing up my phone. Stop sending me a hundred texts a day. Stop trying to push past the armor bearers after Sunday services to get to me. Stop calling my wife from blocked numbers and not saying anything. I don't want to bar you from Holy Rock...but keep messing with me and my family and you'll be sorry."

"I did not call your wife!" Detria seethed. "If she told you that then she's a boldfaced liar," she continued to scream. "And don't you dare make threats to me, Khalil. You don't know who you're messing with!"

"See, this is what I mean. You can't control yourself. You take things too far. Look, you know I'm married now. I can't be seen running around with...with the church h...with you. Or anyone other than my wife for that matter."

"I know you were not about to call me a hoe?" She waved a manicured finger in his face. Khalil pushed it away. "So all of a sudden you're some choir boy or something? You think you're better than me 'cause you married that felon wife of yours."

"I have a kid now, Detria. Just because you don't have anything to do with your kid, well, that's not me."

Detria looked like she'd been slapped. Tears formed but instead of releasing them she began releasing a string of expletives.

"You acting like this lets me know I made the right decision to stop messing with you. You're nothing but some rich hood chick slut. I mean, dang, you were married to my uncle, you slept with my father, and now you're screwing me, his son? Think about it, did you honestly think it could have ever been more than what it was, Dee? I don't mean to be hurtful, but it's the only way I can get you to see that you are *not* the prize. Look, I'm outta here. I just need you to know, again, that it's over. Completely over. Don't call me or my wife ever again. You got that?" Khalil turned and walked out of the family room toward the foyer leading to the front door.

"I can't believe you're doing this," Detria cried, running up behind him. "You can't just walk out of my life like this relationship was nothing. After everything I've done for you, how could you do me like this?"

Khalil kept walking, not bothering to respond or look back. Arriving at the front door, Detria grabbed hold of his arm and jerked him around. “Please, don’t do this, Khalil. Don’t do me like this. I don’t deserve this.”

“Take care of yourself, Dee.” Khalil opened the door and strolled out, not bothering to close it behind him.

Detria cried and wailed. “Khalil, Khalil, come back!” She stood in the doorway until Khalil sped off before she crumbled to the floor in a heap.

Without looking back, Khalil drove off. “Hey,” he spoke aloud in his car, “I’m on my way home. Do you need me to stop and bring anything?” he called and asked Eliana.

“No, but thanks for thinking of us,” she told him.

“That’s what husbands and fathers are for,” he said, smiling. “See you in fifteen.” He stopped along the way and grabbed a dozen red roses from the florist. He was going to go all out to do what needed to be done to secure his marriage whether he was in love with his wife or not.

†

"What's wrong? Did the boys wake up?" Pepper stirred out of her sleep, looking up drowsily at Xavier.

"No, and I'm sorry to wake you, but I've got a call coming in. Business, I have to get this," Xavier briefly explained, easing Pepper out of the crook of his arm after their heated lovemaking.

Pepper turned over, closed her eyes, and went back to sleep.

Rising from their bed, he stepped into his boxers and answered Trevor Price's call. He listened with intensity to the information Trevor shared concerning Hezekiah.

"Do you know who it was that called?" Xavier asked Trevor.

"No idea. It was from a PRIVATE number, and I can't begin to guess why they contacted me and not the authorities. I started not to answer it, but sometimes clients call me from unknown numbers so I picked it up. Man, am I glad I did. The caller said the police need to look at Jude's stepfather. You know what he's talking about? Do you know a kid named Jude? Does Hezekiah have another kid?"

Xavier sighed before answering. Breathing into the phone he remarked, "Yeah…my father has an outside kid. His name is Jude. He's about five or six, I think. Me, my mother and my brother didn't find out about him until some months before my father was shot. It could have something to do with the time when my father gained custody of Jude, although that was for a very short period, a few weeks or so. From what I understand, Dad told the courts he was concerned for his son's safety because Jude's stepfather was a convicted pedophile. He didn't want his kid living around a sex offender. The judge awarded Dad temporary custody until they could do a full investigation. In the end, the courts determined Jude was safe and could go back to his mother. It's a long, crazy story, but I recall Dad saying the stepfather was highly upset. The man may have even lost his job because of that. I'm not sure if Jude's mother stayed with him. Either way, it was nasty for a minute, but to think he would try to kill my father because of it? I don't know about that. People have taken another person's life for things far less serious." Xavier was puzzled.

"Something must have happened and things went south. But after that tip, I think he's worth investigating. In the meantime, I am going to notify the police, let them know what went down."

"I hope this is the break we need," Xavier exclaimed. "If he did shoot my father, he needs to pay."

six

"The power to do good is also the power to do harm." Unknown

Rianna returned to Memphis while Big Daddy remained in Seattle with his wife for a few extra days. At home, Rianna brought in her luggage and then packed a small overnight bag.

"I appreciate you picking me up from the airport," she told Tiny, "and staying around to take me to pick up a rental car."

"Girl, you know it's no problem. I was off work today and the boy is with his daddy. I wasn't gonna do nothing but stop and get me a sandwich and go home and watch my shows. You sure you don't want me to ride with you?"

"Nah, girl, that's too much. You have to be at work tomorrow and I *sho* don't want to get you fired. Especially since I don't know what time I'm going to leave from up there. You know how they are at Walgreens. They don't think nothing about letting one of us go. I sho don't want you putting your job in jeopardy because of me."

"Yeah, I know, but I don't care," Tiny paused. "Nah, that's a lie. I care, but I'm still sick of going to that store every day. Some folks have all the luck," she said, giving Rianna the side eye.

"Girl, please. If you wanted to you could find yourself a sugar daddy or a good man, but you too hung up on your *baby daddy*, and he don't deserve you. Plus, he's got a wife. I mean, I know Big Daddy has a wife too, but it didn't stop me from having a man. How do you think I snagged Hezekiah? It sure wasn't from sitting around giving all my time to Big Daddy. Me and him have an understanding. He has a wife and now I have a husband. He's not going to leave his wife and I don't have to leave Hezekiah." Rianna laughed.

"I know, but I guess he's my bad habit," Tiny said and shrugged.

"Suit yourself."

Tiny dropped Rianna off at the rental car station and Rianna got on the road. From what she had been told the last time she spoke to one of the hospital nurses, Hezekiah had been moved out of ICU and was in a regular hospital room.

The nearly six hour drive left her tired, frustrated, and not in the best of moods. She traipsed into the hospital and went to the floor the woman from the prison had given her.

"I'm here to visit Hezekiah McCoy."

"Prison ID number," the male nurse at the front desk asked.

Rianna looked inside her phone, found the number, and read it off.

The nurse stood up and walked from behind the nurse's station. "Come with me," he said, chewing a piece of gum and popping it.

Rianna ignored his ill manners and followed him down the hall where she was led into a cold, empty dimly lit waiting room with several steel chairs and a flat screen mounted on the wall.

"Wait here. Someone will come and get you and take you to the prisoner. I mean patient," he auto corrected himself then turned and walked out of the room, closing the door behind him.

Rianna pulled out her phone and scrolled through social media. After waiting for about ten minutes or so, she started texting Tiny back and forth.

The door suddenly swung open, hitting the back of the wall, startling Rianna who was entertaining herself by watching TikTok videos in between text exchanges with Tiny.

A man different from the first nurse appeared and ordered, "Come with me."

She scurried her items together and quickly stood, following the *Jack and the Beanstalk* sized nurse, guard, or whatever his job title.

Without further conversation, she trailed behind "Nurse Jack" until they arrived in front of a door that had signs posted. One sign read OXYGEN IN USE. Another sign... FALL RISK and the largest sign....BLEDSOE CORRECTIONAL INMATE.

"Nurse Jack" opened the door and the two of them entered. He ambled toward the bed where Hezekiah lay and began reading the monitors and standing to the opposite side of where Rianna stood.

Hezekiah weakly looked to his right. His eyes locked with Rianna. Almost right away the monitor showed an increase in his blood pressure and heart rate.

"Nurse Jack" scoured at Rianna and then he looked at Hezekiah.

"Are you up to visitors? You don't have to do this, you know."

Hezekiah nodded and deliberately spoke. "Yes."

"Well, okay, but if your pressure continues to spike, I'll have to ask her to leave. Excuse me," he said as he passed Rianna. He stopped at the door and said, "You have ten minutes."

"Okay, let's make this short and sweet," Rianna said just as quick as the man left. "You'll do anything to get attention, won't you?" She continued poking at him with her mean words.

"You are going to pay. God don't like..."

Rianna flung up a hand and swished around to the other side of Hezekiah's hospital bed. She eyed the various tubes he was connected to.

"Shush, ol' man. You'll give yourself another heart attack," she mocked and laughed aloud.

"Never in a million years will I let you destroy my ministry and my life's work. Never," Hezekiah grumbled. "I want you to turn over all my business matters to Stiles. From this point forward, don't you lay another finger on my money. I've already made all this known to Stiles, I don't want you anywhere near Lion's Gate or New Holy Rock. Do you understand me, you finagling evil witch." His voice was weak, but still demanding.

Rianna leaned back, slapped her thigh, and started cackling. "Takes one to know one," she retorted and took a seat in the chair by the window as if his words didn't matter. "But seriously, I don't know if your snitching brother has told you or not, but I've been called to the ministry, and in your absence I'm taking over the role of Senior Pastor of New Holy Rock Ministries. God surely works in mysterious ways, huh?"

"Never," he strained as veins appeared at the base of his throat and traveled to his temples. "You're a wicked woman, Rianna. You're ruthless and you have no morals."

"Dang, why all the name calling? That's no way to talk to your first lady. Oops, I stand corrected, I meant to say that's no way to talk to the Senior Pastor of New Holy Rock." She broke out in laughter again.

Hezekiah frowned, straining to say something but Rianna gave him no time to reply.

"You know what, Hezekiah? I don't understand people like you. I didn't think you were the kind of man who would go against what the good Lord has ordained. If he called *you* to the ministry why can't I have a calling on my life, too?" she further chatted.

Hezekiah continued struggling to speak. Each word seemed to suck energy out of him and his heart seemed to be racing. *Lord, don't let me have another heart attack.*

"You and I both know God ain't called you to *nuthin.* The devil, well I can see that, but God—naw, God wouldn't dare do that." Hezekiah snarled and turned his head away from Rianna. "Get outta here. There's nothing else I have to say, except this one thing."

"My pleasure," Rianna stood up, folded her arms, stood back in her legs and fixated a mean stare at Hezekiah. "Oh, and not that it matters, but what is that *one* thing you wanna say?"

"I'm getting a divorce. You wait and see. You're going to pay for everything you're doing while I'm locked up."

Rianna picked up her purse that she'd placed on the windowsill and strolled to the other side of the bed. Stopping momentarily, she said, "Well, until that day comes and goes you best believe I'm going to enjoy every single solitary moment being First Lady Rianna McCoy." She laughed maniacally, walked up to Hezekiah, kissed him on his forehead, and waltzed out of the hospital room.

seven

"Power will intoxicate the best hearts, as wine the strongest heads. No man is wise enough, nor good enough to be trusted with unlimited power." Colton

The grounds of Holy Rock were immaculately maintained and perhaps well worth the four figures a month landscaping fees. Lush green, healthy trees lined the entrance to the one-mile stretch of road leading to the church. The multi-story modern brick establishment bore a gigantic cross with two smaller crosses, one on each side. The crosses glowed at night and could clearly be seen from miles around. There were several additional buildings on the 90+ acre lot including a youth facility, full gym, and a senior citizens center where free meals were served to seniors. They could also come to the center and enjoy games, crafts and fellowship with other seniors. Another set of buildings housed a private school for pre-school to third grade. Plans were to eventually operate a school from pre-school to grade twelve.

Much had been accomplished under Khalil McCoy's leadership. He had a seemingly loyal and dedicated staff. Now that he was a husband and a new father, he was hungry even more to get rich. So far he was on a pretty good path. His father had become a millionaire, or close to it, being in the ministry. It was a good business for someone like the McCoys who had charismatic personalities that easily drew people to them. It had worked for Hezekiah and Khalil was determined to make it work for him. Unlike Hezekiah, he was going to reach the pinnacle. Khalil was going to be a multi-millionaire mega pastor. The sky was not the limit for him. Khalil McCoy's aspirations went much higher.

He approached the pulpit and the congregation began clapping and shouting praises. Sometimes Khalil felt like a celebrity actor or famous musician. He welcomed the glory from the people.

Khalil's Sunday message was like most of his other messages—it set the congregation on fire. When he followed up in song, the people went wild like they were at a Beyoncé and Jay Z concert.

"According to Solomon, in the book of Proverbs, there are seven things God hates. Eyes that are arrogant, a lying tongue, hands that murder the innocent, a heart that hatches evil plots, feet that race down a wicked track, a mouth that lies under oath, and a troublemaker in the family," Khalil preached while pacing back and forth across the front of the sanctuary, as was his custom. He huffed and puffed like he was about to blow the church house down. He pointed out toward the congregation and continued to preach with fervor. "God hates these things, but remember God loves you. He tells us not to be conformed to this world, but be transformed by the renewing of our minds. Can I get an Amen!"

Eliana sat on her reserved row, raising her hands in the air, shouting praises with almost every word her husband spoke.

From the rear of the church, tucked away in a corner, with her face hidden under a wide-brimmed hat trimmed in rhinestones, sat Detria Graham. "Look at that pretender," Detria mumbled while raising her hands in the air, waving them like she didn't have a care in the world. She took several evil looks at Eliana sitting on the other side of the sanctuary. They both appeared to be trying to out praise the other.

†

Simultaneously, across town at New Holy Rock Ministries, the congregation was in for a Sunday treat. The choir delivered two powerful, soul stirring songs that had some folks standing on their feet, singing along, clapping and swaying.

From the left front of the church, Rianna paraded behind Pastor Stiles and the guest preacher Rianna had invited, a preacher named Reverend Willie Earl Johnston. It was a name that sounded like it was straight from one of those old time churches in *the hood.*

Reverend Johnston looked like he was Iranian with bone straight black hair with streaks of gray and combed to the back of his *Charlie Brown* shaped head. He appeared to be in his late sixties to maybe early seventies. What was striking was that just like Rianna's friend, Abel, Reverend Johnston was a *little* person. Maybe even a tad shorter than Abel's four feet one height. Stiles found it humorous, not because of the preacher's short stature, but the mere fact Rianna thought she could actually step in and take over New Holy Rock. For her to even think it was as simple as having guest preachers grace the pulpit proved that she was not seeing the whole picture of what ministry involved. He would allow her these few moments of fame, but he couldn't wait until Hezekiah knocked her off of her self-appointed pedestal. That would be the day.

Stiles put on his best Christian stance and welcomed the older preacher. Though he'd never heard of the man, he was willing to give him a chance as long as he respected the Word of God in his pulpit. For now, anything to keep the peace and not bring confusion to the church body on this otherwise perfect Sunday morning was what Stiles desired.

At the end of the hour and half long service, after the congregation shook hands with Stiles and the guest preacher, Stiles shuffled out of New Holy Rock.

Getting inside his car, he was stopped by a woman who identified herself as Tiny Newhouse. She said she was a friend of Rianna's. Next to her stood a little boy who looked to be about seven or eight. Stiles had seen her at church a few times, but did not recall her name.

"How are you, Sister Newhouse. How can I help you?"

"Uh, well, I just wanted to tell you how much I enjoy coming here. I was a little, well I guess scared or nervous about coming when Rianna invited me, but I'm glad I did," she said, smiling at him briefly before looking away.

"Your kid?" Stiles asked, and focused on the boy.

"Oh, yes, this is my son, Aiden. Say hello to the pastor, Aiden."

"Hello," the boy said without expression.

"I'm glad you enjoyed the service. I don't recall you joining. Have you?"

"Uh, no, not yet. I've been thinking about it," she said, shyly.

"Well, just know we would love to have you as an official member of New Holy Rock."

Tiny smiled, tightened her grip on her son's hand, and said, "Thank you, Pastor." She paused.

Stiles spoke up. "You think about what I said. We'd love to have you. You and Aiden have a good week. We'll see you at Bible study this week. That is, if you can make it."

"I...I don't know. Sometimes I have to work. But if I don't, I'll be here." With that, Tiny swiftly turned around and nervously waddled off with her son in tow.

Stiles smiled. "At least Rianna brings her friends to church," he said and chuckled at the thought as he put his car in DRIVE and headed out of the church parking lot.

He stopped at a popular soul food buffet, picked up a to-go plate, and then headed home with plans to chill and watch a game or a good movie.

The sky was taking on a dark shade, a sign that it was about to be a downpour. Unlike some people, Stiles welcomed the rain. It gave him a sense of peace. There was no other way to explain it. It was like with the rain came spiritual cleansing, a chance to wash away the sins and wrongs of the day and usher in freshness and newness.

He arrived home. Almost as soon as he stepped inside, his phone started ringing. He retrieved it out of his pocket and saw Fancy's name appear on the screen.

"Hey, what's up, sis?" It was always good to hear from Fancy. She was one of the few people other than Cynthia that he could confide in and truly be himself. Now that he and Victoria were no longer an item, he cherished the times he had a woman to talk to.

He still missed Victoria, but she had been right—she was not made to be a church girl. She loved her worldly freedom too much. It wasn't that she was out doing things that were less than pleasing. She simply enjoyed her own space and solitude. She loved the Lord but she just did not choose to sit in a church day in and day out. That was not her. She made that more than clear to Stiles, and thus brought an end to their relationship.

"I was just checking on you and I wanted to see if you'd heard anything more about Hezekiah."

"I know Rianna went to see him a couple days ago. She said he was out of ICU and was doing pretty good. She said they're thinking about transferring him to the prison infirmary in a day or so."

"Already? Are they sure he's okay?"

"You know how that goes. We don't have a say so either way. We have to leave it in God's hands. He's taken care of him so far and there's no doubt in my heart whatsoever that God is going to keep His hands on Hezekiah. Like you've said, the man has nine lives," Stiles said, laughing into the phone.

Fancy laughed too. "You're right. I just worry about him. That wife of his is, well, I don't have to say it."

"No, you don't," Stiles countered.

"How was that preacher she invited? I intended to be there, but I woke up feeling bad this morning so I decided I needed to stay inside. I don't want to get anybody sick."

"You okay?" Stiles asked, concern ringing in his voice.

"Yea. Just achy and I have a slight fever. I'll be fine. I already took something for it. So tell me, how was service? Who was the preacher Rianna brought in?"

"First, service was actually good. The preacher's name was Willie Earl Johnston out of Tupelo. You heard of him? A man of short stature. I mean that literally."

"Huh? Short stature? Like a *little* person? A dwarf?"

"Yep, exactly. But that doesn't matter because little person or not, I have to give him credit, the man could render a word. He had the church shouting and praising God. We had three people join church. One wanting to be baptized. I have to give it to my sis-in-law, she did good."

"Whoa, don't fall for her shenanigans. That hussy is a modern day Delilah—you should know that. And the way she's running through Hezekiah's money, well that's a whole other story. I know it might be wrong, but I can't stand her."

"You're entitled to your feelings. I'm the last person to judge you or anyone. As much as I hate to admit it, I can feel you on this. Rianna is ruthless, but I still believe her day is coming. God says vengeance belongs to Him. That's all I know and I've never seen Him go against His word."

"True," agreed Fancy. "So let's not give her any more of our time or energy. What are your plans for the rest of the day?"

"Not much. I stopped and got a plate from Maria's Soul Food. You know how they do; they pile your plate with food. It's enough for now and for later. I'll play my game or watch a game, nothing much. I sure hope you feel better."

"Oh, no worries about me. I'm fine. How are Pastor and Sista Josie?"

"They're good. They made it to church today. It's one thing Pastor still enjoys. He may not recognize me or Josie half the time, but he remembers how much He loves the Lord. Going to church is the highlight of his life. As for Josie, I can see Pastor's declining health is taking a toll on her. She looks weary and tired. They have a CNA who comes a few days every week and Pastor goes to Adult Day care three days a week, but Josie still worries about him. She loves that man. He's blessed to have gained a good godly wife after mother died. I believe Audrey loved Pastor, but I don't know if she loved him as much as Pastor loved her. But when I see him and Josie together, I know their union was ordained by God. We just have to keep Josie lifted in prayer. I mean they're both in their late seventies you know."

"I'll do that. Talking about love and relationships, what's going on with you now that it's over between you and Victoria? I sure hate that. I love both of you guys. I know Victoria may not be the ideal church lady you're looking for, but she's still a sweet person."

"That she is," said Stiles. "And remember, it was Victoria's decision to bring things to an end. I can't say I blame her, and I don't. It takes a lot, a special person to put up with a preacher. It's not for just anybody."

"True, I just hope you don't close off your heart anymore, Stiles. Don't let this break up between send you back to that dark place you were in. You had all but turned away from the possibility of falling in love. Please, promise me you'll keep your heart available and receptive for that special woman. You know what the Bible says: He who finds a wife..."

"Don't do that, Fancy. Do not use the Word on me." He laughed.

"A friend's gotta do what a friend's gotta do," Fancy countered and giggled.

eight

"Sometimes being a friend means mastering the art of timing." Octavia Butler

Eliana finished her morning routine of cleaning, preparing fresh blended fruits and vegetables for Khaliyah, and doing a few loads of laundry. She hummed as she went along, making the most use of her time whenever Khaliyah was in a quiet mood.

She returned the vacuum to the closet while singing a song called "With You" by one of her favorite singers, Mariah Carey. *"I don't know what I'm s'posed to do... it's true,"* she went through the house singing.

Her phone interrupted her serenade. "Hey, what's going on, Pepper?" Eliana answered, breathing heavily into the phone.

"Were you busy?" Pepper asked. "Sounds like I caught you at a bad time."

"Girl, please, when am I *not* busy?" she mused. "I have my hands full juggling a husband and a toddler." Eliana forced a laugh. "But it's all good. What's up?"

"You know I understand about having full hands. I don't know how I would manage if

Xavier hadn't brought on a part time nanny to help me with the boys. I'm telling you, she's been a lifesaver."

"Having a nanny is a good thing. I don't think I've gotten to that point, at least not yet. But you have double the trouble so I see why you would need some extra hands. Anyway, what's going on?"

"I'm calling about tomorrow's meeting. Is it still on?"

"Yeah, everything is set. I just don't want no drama, girl, but it looks like it's already started."

"Already started? What does that mean? How can there be drama already? We haven't even started up good, plus this is a ministry for first ladies. We're supposed to be about glorifying God and our spouses."

"I know but it's just some mess trying to get in my way. Don't worry about it. Overall, I think working with other first ladies and women in ministry is going to be good for not only Holy Rock but for first ladies all over the city. I mean, especially since it's not limited to members of Holy Rock."

"That's what I like about it. When you came up with the idea to start a ministry like this, I had to jump on board. I may not be an official first lady, but Xavier works close enough in the ministry as the youth director, so thanks for letting me be part of it. I have to admit, I didn't know if you were going to want me to be part of it since me and Xavier jumped ship and joined New Holy Rock, but you have to know that it wasn't my idea. I mean, I like being under the leadership of Pastor Stiles. He's a great preacher and teacher, but before Hezekiah got sent to prison I was very against joining. Of course, I wanted to follow my husband and support him so that's what I did."

"Girl, you did the right thing. As for Pastor Stiles, you're right. He's a man after God's own heart. I believe he wants what's best for New Holy Rock and for his brother too. I can't say the same about First Lady Rianna. From everything I've seen and heard that one is a force to be reckoned with."

"Yeah, that's what I've heard too. I overhear Xavier and Khalil talking sometimes, not that I'm eavesdropping, but I can't help but hear them sometimes. From what I can tell, she's not in the marriage or in the church for the reasons one might think."

"What do you mean?"

"I think she's out to wipe Hezekiah of all of his assets while he's incarcerated. Think about it, Rianna was a great choir director when she was at Holy Rock and she's good at New Holy Rock too, but she's not the friendliest person. I watch my back whenever I'm around her. I hope she doesn't want to join this new ministry you're starting, *The Pulpit Ladies.*"

"If she does, we can't turn her away. I mean it *is* geared toward first ladies, so if she chooses to come aboard, as along as she behaves according to the guidelines and our bylaws, then we shouldn't be the ones to discriminate or pass judgment. We have to accept her since we're women of God."

"I know, I know, but still she's not to be trusted."

"That I agree with. Look, let me get off this phone. I still have to bathe and dress Khaliyah."

"Sure," Pepper said. "I didn't mean to interrupt."

"You didn't. It's always good talking to you. I'm glad we've established a friendship."

"Yeah, me too. Us mothers have to stick together," she mused.

Eliana chuckled. "Yes, we sure do. So tell you what, we can talk more at the meeting tomorrow. I'm still developing ideas for the ministry so if you come up with something, jot it down and bring the notes with you. There are only going to be five of us tomorrow. I'm depending on y'all to help me work out the best plans for the ministry. Oh, I almost forgot. I'm going to serve a light lunch. You know, finger sandwiches, some of those mini quiches, a fruit tray, mimosas and soda pop. Nothing fancy."

"That sounds good. I can bring some chips and a bowl of my homemade ranch dip if you'd like."

"Yes, that would be perfect. Thanks!"

"No thanks necessary. See you tomorrow."

"Oh, before I forget, babies are welcome," Eliana said, giggling.

Pepper giggled too. "Perfect. Okay, buh-bye."

Pepper was happier than she'd been in a long time, since before she got pregnant. She still thought about her little girl who died during birth, but seeing her boys growing into rambunctious toddlers was a blessing she was grateful and appreciative of.

Almost a year and a half had gone by since she and Xavier got back together and she had returned to their home. In her eyes her marriage seemed stronger. She didn't question her husband about Ian. From what she'd heard through Eliana, Ian had moved out of Memphis. Finding that out was a huge relief for Pepper. With Ian out of the picture, it made things easier for her and Xavier's marriage to have a chance.

She made a promise not to bring up her husband's sexuality or anything pertaining to his former relationships. As long as he was satisfying her sexually, putting forth an effort to be a good husband and father, she convinced herself his past was just that – the past. There were times however when she felt like he was struggling to keep his desire for men under control, but she didn't believe he'd stepped out on their marriage. She often told herself during times of doubt, if God could forgive Xavier, then who was she to hold his past sins and transgressions against him. She prayed each day for God to keep Xavier's eyes on her and not on some man. So far, it appeared that God had answered her prayers.

nine

"He who searches for evil must first look at his own reflection." Confucius

Eliana threw a hand to her head in frustration. "Dang, who could it be now? I'm not expecting anybody," she said, looking at a bright-eyed Khaliyah like the little girl understood what she was saying.

She rushed to the door as the doorbell rang a second followed by a third.

"Just a minute," she yelled, holding her daughter on one hip.

Exhaling, she opened the door and right away her eyes gawked at the huge bouquet of roses. Only her look was not one of happiness but one of curiosity mixed with an uneasy feeling growing in the pit of her belly.

"Yes," she said when she saw the man standing on the other side with the bouquet.

"Eliana...uh, Eliana McCoy?" he said, studying the note card he held in his hand.

"Yes, I'm Eliana." She remained fixated on the roses with eyebrows lifted and head slightly tilted as Khaliyah struggled to reach the bouquet.

"No, no, baby," she said, pulling back her daughter's chubby hand.

"These are for you," the polite young man announced. He gave the vase of roses to a puzzled Eliana.

"Who are they from?"

"There should be a card attached, ma'am."

"Uh...oh, okay. Th...thank you." She accepted the bouquet with her free hand while still holding her daughter back from grabbing a thorned rose.

The young man turned and left as Eliana backed back a step and closed the door with one foot.

She went into the kitchen and placed the vase on the counter before taking Khaliyah into the family room and putting her in her pack 'n play.

Going back into the kitchen, she searched through the bouquet for a note.

"Who in the devil would send me a bouquet of roses, and black roses too?"

Searching through the at least two or more dozen of black roses, she squealed as thorns nipped her fingers, bringing forth bits of blood. She soon found a card tucked away deep inside the bouquet. Opening it, she read the note and was instantly livid. "Do not underestimate the things I will do," the note read. No one had signed it. Eliana looked through the bouquet again. There was nothing else there.

As if that wasn't enough, suddenly she heard a loud commotion outside. "What in the world?" She hurried back to the front door.

Her mouth went agape and her eyes stretched wide when she opened her front door and saw Detria Graham sitting in her car with her hand pressing on her car horn. This *wanch* is crazy for real," Eliana said, biting down on her lip.

Detria let up on the horn and then started screaming threats when Eliana appeared at the door. "Khalil is mine. He doesn't want you. It's only a matter of time before that kid won't keep him home. He's coming back to my bed," she screamed.

"You are crazy," Eliana yelled back while standing on her porch. "And if you don't get off my property I'm calling the police." Eliana came further down the steps.

"Call whoever you want. I'll be gone by the time they get here. Anyway, you get my drift," Detria threatened again. "Enjoy the roses. You know the saying, give them their flowers while they live," Detria mocked and started laughing as she sped off.

"You betta get your behind off of my property and don't you ever come back!" Eliana warned, running behind the car like an Olympic track star.

Detria's tires burned rubber against the pavement as the dark blue Infiniti Q50 sped off.

Eliana continued waving her arms as the car disappeared from sight. Finally, after Detria was out of her sight, Eliana turned, folded her arms, and dashed back inside the two-story brick colonial.

Running up the porch steps, she heard her baby crying as she stepped inside the huge foyer.

"Good lord, what was I thinking? Here I come, sweetheart," she yelled, running down the hallway and around the corner to her crying baby girl.

She dashed inside, swooped Khaliyah out of her pack 'n play, and began kissing and hugging on the precious little one. Whispering sweet words, the baby calmed down and nestled her head against her mother's shoulder.

"Mommy's sorry," she cooed and almost immediately little Khaliyah calmed down.

"The nerve of her showing up at our home!" Eliana swore out loud. "And to send me black roses, too. Yeah, that trick has gone too far, Khaliyah." She kissed her daughter's rosy cheek again.

She went and retrieved her cell phone off the kitchen countertop. Scrolling through her CONTACTS, she stopped when she found the number for their community's HOA office and called it. When the pleasant sounding woman answered, Eliana told her about her dilemma and asked them to make sure they ramped up the drive through security in her area. She gave her a description of Detria's car. The woman assured Eliana she had noted her complaint and would make sure she passed it on to the community's Security Department.

She ended that call and then proceeded to call Khalil. Juggling the baby in one arm and resting her on her hip, she called Khalil.

"What is it?" Kahlil asked, removing his lean legs from the top of his desk and resting both feet on the cushioned carpet.

"I can't take it anymore," Eliana screamed into the phone.

"Hol' up! What's going on? Is my daughter all right?"

"Yes, Khaliyah's good. It's me. I'm the one that's not all right. That crazy woman sent me dozens of black roses, and then on top of that she just left our home, Khalil. She's a lunatic and you keep letting her get away with disrespecting me and disrespecting our home! But she's gone too far this time; I'm calling the police."

"What are you talking about?" Khalil asked, knowing she couldn't be talking about anyone other than Detria. Even though he had called things off between them, Detria still had been doing stupid stuff like blowing up his phone with text messages and threatening calls. Now this. "Look, I'll handle it."

"You better handle it. How did she even get inside our neighborhood? We live in a gated community. I don't understand. I'm going to put a restraining order against her if you can't handle her."

"I told you...I got it. Look, I gotta go. I have a staff meeting about to take place. I'll hit you back later. Now chill out and kiss my daughter for me."

†

Detria practically howled, overcome with laughter, as she sped off, commandeering the car with her one good arm. Losing the use of an arm hadn't affected her in the least bit when it came to driving.

"Girl was running behind this car like a Sha'Carri Richardson clone," she talked to herself.

Detria kept laughing and shaking her head as she continued speeding up the street and out into the main intersection. Almost instantly, as she sped through the yellow light, she eyeballed the approaching police cruiser from her inside rear view mirror. "Dang it!" she yelled when she saw his lights start flashing. She slowed down while constantly glancing in the mirror.

She continued driving for another block until she was able to safely pull over to the curb. She took another lingering look to see if the police officer had gotten out of his car.

"Ok, ok, here he comes," Detria mumbled and quickly began patting her hair and glanced in the mirror to check her lips. Rummaging through her purse, she pulled out a tube of MAC lipstick, opened it, and refreshed her thick lips.

"Ummm, he doesn't look bad," she mused and pushed the button to release the driver's side window. "Actually, he's sorta cute."

Watching through the outside mirror, she sized up the uniform coming toward her car.

"Ma'am," the *Terrance Howard* lookalike acknowledged as he positioned his muscular physique in front of her door, "do you know why I pulled you over?"

"Uh, because you want to ask me out to dinner," Detria quipped, her hazel brown contacts going up and down the length of the officer like he was a delicious bowl of ice cream, especially when she quickly noted he wore no ring on his left hand.

Seemingly not amused, the officer remained professional in his response. "You were going fifty in a thirty-five mile an hour zone. License and registration please."

"Of course. My registration is in my glove compartment. May I?" Detria asked, looking at the officer before pointing to her glove compartment.

The officer nodded.

Detria removed the plastic binder that held her car papers, including her registration. Next, she looked inside her designer purse, removed her matching wallet, and retrieved her driver's license.

"Here you go, uhh..." Detria leaned her head slightly out the window and looked up at the officer's badge. "Officer Clark."

"Didn't you see the sign back there?"

Detria smiled, flashing her long faux mink lashes at the officer. "No, officer, I'm so sorry, I didn't. I was trying to get to the school to pick up my son. His father, my *ex*," she emphasized the lie, "was supposed to pick him up, but he didn't show up...again. I just got a call from the school. I didn't want to leave him standing outside alone," Detria pleaded, glancing at the officer.

The officer pulled out his ticket pad and began writing as if not paying attention to her explanation.

"I'll give you a break. I'm writing a ticket for you going 40 miles instead of 50. Anything more than five miles over the speed limit can increase your insurance." His voice was sultry and baritone.

Detria flashed her lashes again. "Thank you, Officer Clark. Thank you so much."

He nodded, gave Detria the ticket, and followed with, "You be careful out here, ma'am," finally cracking an almost unnoticeable smile, but not before Detria caught a glimpse of it.

The officer turned and started walking off.

"Hey, Officer Clark," called Detria as he arrived at his cruiser.

"Yes, ma'am?"

"What about that dinner? It's on me." She flirted.

The officer smiled and got inside his car. Pulling off, he nodded and smiled as he passed.

ten

"Life is a series of natural and spontaneous changes. Don't resist them – that only creates sorrow." Lao Tzu

Fancy and Victoria turned into Lion's Gate. Fancy used her gate FOB to gain entrance into the secluded neighborhood.

Victoria drove her cherry red Lexus truck pass sculptured manicured lawns and massive homes that made the Lion's Gate neighborhood a refuge for some of the city's upper middle class. Living behind the gate was a show of status and prosperity.

Nestled in the midst of Whitehaven just blocks from Graceland, once behind the gates, one might think they had been catapulted into another world. There was an Olympic sized salt water indoor/outdoor pool with a 5,500 square feet clubhouse, several pool houses, a fine dining restaurant, a quaint quick food café, neighborhood store, tennis and basketball courts, fitness room, and a number of other amenities.

The day was almost perfect. It was a beautiful Saturday afternoon in the mid-fifties, sun out, a slight breeze, and clear skies.

"When was the last time you ran into your arch nemesis?" Victoria asked as she continued driving.

"Don't talk that crazy woman up. But to answer your question, I haven't seen her inside these gates since before Hezekiah went to prison. I don't make a habit of going on her street, of course. And I've never seen her at the clubhouse, pool or anything, not that I go there often."

"I'm just glad she's staying out of your way."

"What you say, me too. Other than seeing her when I go to New Holy Rock, which is rare, I don't think about her. Well, I do think about her, but I'm telling you they're not good thoughts. I hate the way she's taking advantage of Hezekiah being in prison to live her best life. I know he's done some unsavory things in his life, but he doesn't deserve to have someone like Rianna destroy him the way she's trying to do. Uhh, I wish she'd just disappear. You know, move out of Memphis. Leave him alone," Fancy lamented.

Victoria continued driving until minutes later she turned onto Fancy's street. She pulled into the driveway and the ladies remained in the car and continued talking.

"She's like a dripping faucet that you can't turn off. She drives me crazy. I can only imagine what Hezekiah must be going through knowing she's spending every penny of his money she can get her greedy claws on and there's nothing he can do about it. I feel so bad for him."

Victoria looked at Fancy and patted her friend's hand. "I know it's not fair, but don't worry, she's going to have her day. You wait and see. As for Hezekiah, it's no secret you still love him. I can hear it in your voice and see it on your face."

"No, it's not that I still love him, but he's the father of my sons. The man has been in my life since we were teenagers. We've been through hell and high water together," she explained as they walked toward her house. "But am I still in love with him? I don't think so. He's done some awful things to me, to the boys. For goodness sakes, Vicky, the man has a kid out there, a six or seven year old kid! And me, *ooohhhhh* stupid, naïve li'l ol' me didn't find out about it until all this mess came up. And you do know he slept with his brother's wife, right?"

"Who *are* you talking about?" Victoria then asked, tilting her head slightly and raising a brow.

"Detria Graham is who I'm talking about. Hezekiah slept with her."

Victoria appeared shocked. Her complexion turned tomato red. She opened her car door and stood outside.

Fancy got out the car and spoke as she walked. "Don't look so baffled. You heard me right. Did you forget he's the one who set me up with Winston without me knowing? Can you imagine how I felt when I found out he was being paid to go after me by Hezekiah? How psycho was that? And everybody thinks I still love him? I would be a fool. Look at how he up and married that tramp. Okay, so after everything I just said, why do I still care about him? Something's wrong with me, Vicky."

They talked while Fancy unlocked the front door, frowned, went inside and went to the hallway mirror where she stared at her reflection with disappointment.

Victoria followed and posted behind her. "Stop it. Nothing's wrong with you. You're human. Okay, so he's done some terrible things, but you're a good person." She rested her hands on Fancy's shoulders. "You care about his well-being, that's all."

"Yes, you're right. I care about his well-being," Fancy whispered.

"I didn't mean to make you relive all of that. I'm sorry."

"Don't be." Fancy turned to her friend and they affectionately embraced.

Fancy stepped back and they smiled at each other.

Composed again, Fancy started the conversation up again. “Stiles said Hezekiah’s going to file for divorce, something he should have done a long time ago. Heck, he shouldn’t have ever married her. I don’t know what he was thinking.”

“You know Hezekiah better than anyone. You know everything he does he does for a reason. Maybe he thought he could really trust her. But turned out she’s good at the game she plays. A real life walking, talking, breathing Delilah mixed with a little Jezebel.”

“That’s an understatement. She’s definitely on her game. Thing is, Hezekiah is usually a pretty good judge of character. I don’t know what happened this time, but she pulled the blinders all the way over his eyes. I have to say it even though I don’t want to admit it, but I think he met his match when he met Rianna Jamison. Come on, let’s go inside and have that glass of wine and watch some TV.”

“Let’s do it,” Victoria agreed.

Inside Fancy’s house, they were greeted by a beautiful blue point Siamese cat, Fancy’s new addition to her single household.

“I still cannot believe you went and got a cat, of all things. What were you thinking?”

Victoria asked as she watched Fancy go about the kitchen preparing the cat's food.

"I've always loved animals. But I never had one after me and Hezekiah got married. It was going to be too much trying to take care of a pet the way it needed to be taken care of and running around doing all the daily things we needed to do to raise the boys and work in the ministry. From taking them to soccer, basketball, football, and whatever else we could get them into, we did it, and that wasn't including all the time we spent at church. Taking care of a pet wasn't in the cards, but I always said I was going to get a dog or cat after the boys were grown and gone. As for cats, I prefer them over dogs because they don't require someone to always be in their face. They mess with you on their own terms and their terms only."

Fancy retrieved two wine glasses while Victoria pulled out a bottle of Mosato Red from the fridge. The ladies left out of the kitchen, leaving the cat to enjoy his dinner.

"Speaking of me having a cat, he's good company. He helps me during those times when I'm sitting here feeling sorry for myself. He'll come up and put his cold little nose against me or rub his fat face on me, and I melt. It soothes me in a way," Fancy explained while the ladies sat in the family room sipping on their glasses of wine.

"That makes sense. We all need something or somebody to love, whether it's an animal or a human," added Victoria. "I like animals, but I know I don't have time to take care of them and you know me, I value my freedom. I want to be able to get up and go when I want to. I want to go on a trip when I want to and not have to worry about having to board my pet or get somebody to pet sit."

The cat appeared and jumped up in Fancy's lap. "Do you miss Stiles?" Fancy asked, rubbing Sebastian with one hand and holding the glass of wine in the other.

"Of course, but not enough that I regret breaking things off. I've learned over the course of my life, especially after my divorce from Pepper's father, that I have to be true to me. As much as I adored Stiles, maybe even loved him, I was not going to settle for being anybody's First Lady. That's not who I am. Other than him being a pastor, Stiles is a great guy. He's just not the man for me and I'm not the woman for him. Plain and simple."

"I wish it was that simple for me, but it's not. I still can't believe how I let some guy like Winston come into my life and fool my panties off. I was so naïve and stupid. A full grown woman and yet I fell for the first man who stepped up to me after my divorce. Wow. What was I thinking? No wonder Hezekiah was able to manipulate me all those years of our marriage."

"Don't do that, Fancy. We've all played the fool sometimes. You, me, Hezekiah, Stiles, all of us. Nobody gets a pass in this thing called life. We all fall down and hopefully we get up again. It's like a vicious cycle. We all mess up, make mistakes, and do or say things we later regret. But I'm telling you this one thing; I am *not* going to walk around like I used to do and beat up on myself. I stopped doing that after my divorce. I learned how to forgive myself and you have to do the same thing. As for you and Hezekiah, if you still have feelings for him, don't worry about what me or anyone else has to say. Do what makes you happy. The only person you have to answer to is yourself and the good Lord."

"And that's the way I like it."

eleven

"Do not let what you cannot do interfere with what you can do." John Wooden

Khalil was satisfied that he had delivered another good sermon. He welcomed a number of new members to Holy Rock at each of the three Sunday services. After church, he, Eliana and Khaliyah had their afternoon meal at one of the restaurants he and Eliana frequented after church.

Pulling into the driveway of their home after eating, he got out of the car and carried Khaliyah inside.

"Here's your mommy," he said to the little girl who reached for Eliana.

Eliana eagerly welcomed her daughter.

"Hey, I need to run back to the church. I left something in my office. I'll be right back."

"Can't whatever you left wait until tomorrow?" she asked. Her tone was short and the tense lines that suddenly appeared on her face told him she was not a happy camper.

"Nah, I need to go back. I left my tablet. I'm going to need it later this evening."

Eliana sighed and Khaliyah started pulling on her mommy's bottom lip and gave her sloppy kisses all over her face. Eliana's frown turned into a smile and then a giggle.

Khalil used the positive moment to follow up by giving his wife a peck on the cheek, and then darted out the door back to the garage. He hated that he lied to his wife, but he wasn't about to tell her his real destination. No way.

Not long after leaving the house, he stood outside Detria Graham's house, pounding on her door. She obviously thought he wasn't serious about her leaving him alone. He had to make sure she understood that she was playing a dangerous game.

Expecting Dee, he was unpleasantly surprised when Priscilla answered the door.

"Hi, Pastor Khalil. Uh, Detria's not home yet. Didn't you see her at church?"

"No, I didn't but I wasn't looking for her either," he said with a deep frown creasing his otherwise smooth brown melanin skinned face. "Anyway, what I have to say is not to be said at church. Look, Priscilla, I need you to do me a favor."

Priscilla eyed him curiously. "A favor? What kind of a favor?"

"I need you to tell Detria to back off, leave me and my family alone. I've warned her and I've tried being reasonable with her, but she insists on harassing my wife and making a scene. If she keeps this up, I'm going to have her locked up."

"I'll talk to her, *Pastor*," Priscilla emphasized. "But you're a man of God. You know what the good book says—

"What specifically are you talking about, Priscilla?" Khalil sounded puzzled.

"You reap what you sow. You have to turn from your wicked ways and do what the Lord says. 'Specially you, Pastor Khalil. You being in a position of leadership and authority. You have a lot on your shoulders. You bear the burden of leading folks astray. Now I don't mean to sound disrespectful but you know what you and Dee been doing is wrong. It's wrong before God. You know that child loves you. I didn't say it was right, but it's your doing. You know you didn't mean her no good, yet you came up in here night after night, day after day, sleeping with her, lying to her, and taking advantage of her feelings for you. A real man of God wouldn't have done those things," Priscilla chastised.

"Look, you're right, but I'm not here for all that right now, Priscilla. I'm here because I've told Detria to stay out of my life and leave me and my family alone. I'm trying to do right; whether you think I should have done this a long time ago doesn't matter. I'm doing it now," he emphasized. “Okay, so I may have done wrong, but I’m here now and I’m telling you to talk to her. I asked God to forgive me for the things I’ve done. I told Dee I was going to be with my family, but she won’t accept it and I’ve had enough.”

“I’ll be sure to tell her,” Priscilla said without expressing the least bit of emotion. “Now, if that’s all, I have to get back to my duties.”

Standing momentarily in silence, he then said, “Yes, that’s all, Priscilla.” Waving a slight hand in defeat, he walked off the porch paraded toward his car.

Detria arrived as he about to get in his car. She hurriedly got out of the car and raced toward him, happy Khalil had come.

Standing face to face he blasted her out for coming to his home and for sending the bouquet of black roses to his wife. “Are you crazy?” he yelled and flailed his hands while Priscilla stood in the doorway unashamedly listening and watching.

“You shouldn’t ignore me then,” Dee screamed back. “You know how crazy I get when I think I’m being ignored,” she cooed and stepped toward him, only for Khalil to shove her back, causing her to stumble and almost fall, but she managed to stay upright.

"I love you, Khalil. I told you that. After everything I've done for you, you want to cast me aside like yesterday's garbage? How could you? How could you do me like this?"

"Look, crazy lady. You knew from the start that what we had was nothing. Honestly, do you think I would want to be with a woman who was married to my uncle, had a baby with his best friend, then slept with my father, and now you're sleeping with me?" he said, raising both hands and shaking his head in disbelief. "Where exactly did you think this was going to end up, Dee? I do *not* love you," he said with venom. "You certainly didn't think me and you would be walking down some aisle or spending forever together." He chuckled. "No way. You know what you were to me —a chick on the side. Nothing more. Don't get it twisted."

Detria stood in front of him, tears began cascading down her face as she listened to Khalil's biting words. Her anger grew with every word he spoke. It was like he was stabbing her over and over again. She rushed him again, but this time instead of trying to give him kisses, she started pounding him in his chest repeatedly and then tried to scratch him with her long claw like nails.

Priscilla rushed out the door and ran toward her. "Detria, no! Stop," she cried out.

Khalil shoved her again while releasing a barrage of expletives and grabbing hold of her arm and twisting it.

Detria landed on the concrete pavement, still crying.

Priscilla pushed him to the side and hovered over the crying, hysterical Detria.

"Get away from here!" Priscilla screamed at Khalil. "Leave now or I'm calling the police."

"Gladly!" Khalil retorted. "Go ahead, call the police. See who'll go to jail. You best believe it won't be me. I'm telling you this one last time," he pointed at Dee, "leave me and my family alone!"

Lashing out, Dee yelled while Priscilla helped her to her feet, "And what if I don't...what if I don't?" she repeated.

Khalil stormed off, got to his car, and stood at the open door and warned, "You'll be sorry," before he got in his car and drove off.

Inside the house, Priscilla confronted Detria. "You're going to keep on until you end up in serious trouble. You've got to stop this foolishness. Running up behind a man ain't good. I'm telling you what I know. And a married one at that."

"You don't understand, Priscilla. I love him," Detria cried.

"You shouldn't be involved with someone else's husband. It's not right." Priscilla shook her head as she pounded off. "It just ain't right."

Detria took off in the opposite direction and bolted up the stairs. Inside her bedroom, she flung herself across the bed and cried.

†

"Crazy woman," Khalil mouthed as he pushed 90 on the interstate. Driving fast was a way for him to release pinned up stress and he was certainly stressed after his encounter with Detria. He looked in his rear view mirror, trying to make sure she hadn't scratched him or left visible marks. The last thing he needed was to go home and Eliana saw that he'd been in a fight or something.

He called Omar. He had a way of making Khalil see reason. He had talked him off a ledge many times so he pushed the button and waited for his best friend to answer. He released another round of expletives as the phone started ringing.

"What's up, amigo?" Omar answered.

"Man, I know you're probably just getting home from church, but I'm so heated. I had to call somebody, bruh."

"Hey, no problem. I'm still at church. It takes a minute to make sure everything is closed down and turned off, you know. I should be done soon. What's going on?"

"Man, I just went a round with that crazy girl, Dee. Man, she keeps trying me, Omar."

"What did she do this time, amigo?"

Khalil told him how Dee had shown up at his home and that she had sent dozens of black roses to Eliana. "I'm telling you, she's gone too far, Omar. I couldn't take it so I went over there right after church. It took everything in me not to lay hands on ol' girl."

"I hope you didn't do that, man," Omar replied.

"Nah, I said it took everything in me not to. She had me that hot. I don't believe in hitting on women, but I'm telling you, I was heated, man."

"I don't know what to tell you other than to stay as far away from her as you can. I would tell Eliana to do the same. The only other solution I see is you may have to get a restraining order. It's the only way to handle it legally. You got too much to lose, my friend."

"Yeah, I've gotta do something. I don't want to hurt her, but she's pushing all my buttons. I'm ready to go clean off, and that I don't want to do. I swear she don't want to see that side of me."

twelve

"Never give up, for that is just the place and time that the tide will turn." Harriet Stowe

Rianna hummed then switched to outright singing as she paraded out of Apartment 3D. Rarely did she stop by the apartment.

Apartment 3D, thanks to Abel's suggestion, had turned into a decent side hustle for Rianna with her renting it out as an Airbnb. There were some days and nights she stayed at the apartment herself, but that was because some things she felt more at ease doing behind the doors of Apartment 3D rather than Lion's Gate. Such as entertaining men she met on her favorite dating app.

Driving along the stretch of highway toward Lion's Gate, she thought about how much her life had changed. The upside about Hezekiah's crib was the privacy she enjoyed living behind the gate. It was like living in a whole other world. A world where she had just about everything a girl could desire at her disposal. Except for what she wanted most—a shopping mall.

She laughed at herself at the thought of a shopping mall inside Lion's Gate. "I would be their biggest customer," she said, giggling before switching to more serious thoughts.

In her eyes, God had brought her a mighty long way. Growing up, she'd been shuffled from foster home to foster home, sometimes where she was subjected to living with less than loving people. Other times, she was dragged off to church Sunday after Sunday, two or three times a week. She was often reminded of what a dirty little girl she was and that she needed to constantly repent for the sins of her parents.

The good thing Rianna gained from going to church was how it seemed that the wife of the preacher who was called the First Lady was always looked up to and treated like royalty. Rianna would often daydream during church and at her foster home of one day being a First Lady. Now look at her. Here she was today. Her dream had come true.

Inside the house at Lion's Gate, she showered and shampooed her natural locs.

Stepping outside the shower onto the heated tile floor, she grabbed an oversized towel, wrapped it around her trim body, and ventured inside the custom walk-in closet that housed countless dresses, pant sets, and shoes, many with the tags still on them.

"I need something special for Big Daddy. Hmm." She started singing again as she shuffled through outfit after outfit, only to end up shuffling away discontent. "Nothing in here will work."

She dolled herself up so she could go buy the three piece pant set she'd seen earlier in the week at one of the stores she frequented. When she finished getting dressed, she texted Tiny. Seeing that it was Wednesday, Tiny's usual day off, maybe she would ride with her.

"At work. Filling in for Chassidy, that new chick that transferred from the West Memphis store. She called off sick…again. Girl, she ain't even been here a month!"

"Girl, some folks don't care 'bout nothing," Rianna texted back. "She's one of 'em. Can't believe they ain't fired her."

"IKR dang I wish I had told 'em I couldn't come in, then again I can use the xtra hours."

"I'll stop by after I'm done," she texted Tiny. "Maybe by the time I'm finished you can take lunch or a break, somethin'.

"k, but call or text before you drive all the way over here tho. Just to be sure I can get away."

"Okay, ttyl."

Another text came in before Rianna could put her phone down.

"Change of plans. Staying here rest of week. maybe longer. Will let you know when I'm headed back that way. Abel."

Rianna sighed and instead of texting Abel back, she dialed his number.

"You have reached....."

Before the message was completed, Rianna pressed END as hard as she could with the ball of her index finger. "Ugh, what are you up to, Abel?"

"Change of plans. I'm staying home. Abel not comin. Call when you get off work," she texted Tiny.

"k," Tiny quickly replied.

Rianna paced the floor. Without much thought she scrolled through her phone until she stopped at the number she recalled was the hospital's number where Hezekiah was. When the operator answered, Rianna asked for the prison floor nurses' station. After several minutes, a woman answered.

"That inmate has been transferred back to the correctional facility," the woman informed Rianna.

"Are you sure? No one called and told me. Someone was supposed to keep me informed about his health and certainly that he was transferred back to prison," she snapped.

"Look, ma'am; my shift just started. All I can tell you is he was discharged, uhh last night or early this morning."

"Ok, can you—"

Silence.

"Hello." Rianna eyed her phone before placing it on the marble topped table next to her bedroom door. "You sorry azz...ugh."

She texted Big Daddy. After several minutes, she noticed he had not responded.

"What's going on with him? Guess his wife has him hemmed up." She laughed and then went into the kitchen and poured a glass of wine.

Later on Tiny called and told her she would be over after work.

When Tiny arrived, the two friends laughed and talked, drank wine, ordered takeout, and watched a couple of shows.

"What's up with you and Puff Daddy?" Tiny joked.

"Don't play," Rianna rebuffed. "Big Daddy has it going on. But seriously, I don't know what's up with him lately. He's still in Seattle and he hasn't replied to any of my texts since he said he wasn't coming. I don't know what's going on."

"Could there be trouble in paradise?" Tiny suggested.

"Yeah, maybe. But it's still not like him." Rianna shrugged.

"Don't worry; he'll call or maybe he'll just show up. You never know."

"Right."

"What about your husband. Is he still in the hospital?"

"Girl, nah. I thought he was, but I called the hospital earlier and they said he was transferred back to prison. Keep in mind, no one bothered to pick up the phone to call and tell me. Some folks are so rude," she complained.

"Most folks don't give a darn about inmates. I know firsthand. So what I'm saying is, if you think somebody was going to care enough to call and let you know he was sent back, then you see what you got."

Rianna threw up a hand, then picked up her glass of wine and took a deep swallow before sitting it down and reaching for her barbeque sandwich. "Girl," she said while chewing her food, "their food never fails. It's always fresh and delicious, and the seasoning is to die for."

"Yeah, you got that right," Tiny agreed, taking a big bite of her sandwich as well before propping her legs on the ottoman in front of her. “What is that fine brotha-n-law of yours up to since you won’t let the man preach no mo.” Tiny laughed.

Rianna joined in the laugher. “I’m not keeping him from preaching. I’ve only had guest preachers come in for the past three Sundays and twice during midweek service. What’s wrong with that?”

“Who you think you talking to? I ain’t *boo boo* the fool. You know darn well you intentionally keeping that man out the pulpit. Next, you’ll be telling me you’re going to get up there and preach.” Tiny laughed, took the last swallow from her wine followed by another bite of her sandwich and a couple of her onion rings.

Rianna’s eyes popped wide open like she’d just seen a monster. “Whoa, you just confirmed something that’s been on my mind.” Rianna nodded as if she was coming into agreement with Tiny.

Tiny eyed her friend and rolled her eyes, “No, no, no. Don’t even think about it, Rianna.”

thirteen

"Life always offers you a second chance. It's called tomorrow." Unknown

Hezekiah lay back on his steel bunk reading his Bible. He was preparing to start his Sunday services again. He was feeling better physically, but mentally he had been fighting depression ever since the heart attack 21 days prior. Immediately following his transfer, he went into a funk. He read or heard somewhere that depression following a heart attack was quite common. Learning that seemed to further the slump he was in. On the insistence of some of the inmates who attended his Sunday service, he latched back on to the idea. This Sunday would be the first service since his heart attack.

He put his Bible to the side and opened the hidden compartment he'd made in the brick part of the cell wall, pushed back another block and *oo-lah* his cell phone. He twisted his huge hand inside and finagled it out of the space. Turning the flip phone on and checking to make sure it had a good charge, he called Rianna. Of course, she didn't answer. He followed up with a text. Again, she didn't reply. Why was he not surprised—he hadn't heard from her since her ten minute hospital visit a month ago.

Next, he called his brother. Maybe Stiles could tell him what Rianna was up to. It had been days since he'd called Stiles, but again, depression had a hold of him and the mere thought of talking to someone seemed to make him sick. That, plus prison cries, chatter, the horrific stench 24/7, add a heart attack to that mixture, and Hezekiah was surprised that he'd made a full recovery.

"I know I don't have to tell you, but I'm letting you know anyway that I'm praying for you constantly. New Holy Rock is praying for you. You have to fight against this depressed mindset. You have God on your side. You will overcome this," Stiles shared.

Hezekiah lightly chuckled, but his heart wasn't in hearing his brother's advice, not today. Maybe this feeling would fade over time. Hopefully, forcing himself to restart Sunday service would be good for him more than the inmates that participated.

"Thanks for the support as always, li'l brother. But enough of talking about me and my problems. What's up with you? I know you get tired of me asking, but I'm going to ask anyway. Who you doing?"

What are you talking about?"

"Man, don't play. You know darn well what I'm talking about. I don't understand how, or I should say *why* you still walking around going without." Hezekiah laughed and jumped down off his bunk, landing upright on the concrete floor.

He stood in the cramped cell space, cuffed the phone underneath the side of his face, positioned himself in front of the gray toilet, and took a leak.

"Nah, what's not natural is we out here having sex like it's nothing, no commitment, no expectations, nothing. Been there done that, you know."

"I hear ya, brotha."

"That's not to say I haven't been propositioned by some New Holy Rock groupies. They don't look too bad either." Stiles chuckled, walked to the kitchen, and retrieved a fruit punch out of the fridge. Twisting the cap open, he turned the bottle up to his lips, and took a swig.

"I knew it," Hezekiah said. "A single, half way decent looking guy like yourself, and you're a pastor, drive a fancy car, and have a little change in your pockets...you're the fantasy catch for a lot of ladies out there. Not all of 'em thirsty or bad either, you know."

"I know. I know, but I'm not going to get caught up like that. This time around I'm going to be more careful. I need a lady who's going to be down with me and my ministry. That's why I'm glad Victoria told me her true feelings, that she wasn't cut out for being with a preacher. It's not like I didn't know it, but I guess I didn't want to acknowledge it. She's a good girl though."

"I hear you; she may be a good girl, but she's not the girl for you. That doesn't rule out that you're still a man. You have needs and not just sexual needs. You need a woman. I tell you, I don't know what I'm going to do if I can't get next to a female for the next twenty years. Heck, nah, I got to get outta here."

"You will. Just keep the faith."

"I'm trying, but as for you, I hope you take my advice. You're not locked up. You can find yourself a good woman. Look, I have to go. I'll call you next week and let you know how Sunday service turned out."

"I already know it's going to be good. I'm proud of you doing your ministry, even behind bars."

"This is where it's needed more than ever. You wouldn't believe the things I see and hear. Yeah, God is needed up in here."

"Later, Hezekiah."

"Later, brother. Blessings to ya."

†

Sunday swiftly rolled back around. Once again, Stiles remained in the background while another one of Rianna's guest preachers was supposed to deliver the sermon.

The minister who spoke at midweek service was quite different from the last three guest ministers Rianna conjured up. Stiles actually cringed at hearing some of the non-biblical made up stuff the guy *preached* about. At the end of his ten minute rant, he opened the doors for donations for his ministry rather than offering people to come to Christ. This was one of those times Stiles *turned the other cheek* and remained quiet. But nothing could prepare him for today's preacher, not even the midweek charlatan.

Stiles applauded the choir for their selections, said the welcoming prayer and then like he'd done for the past three Sundays and two midweek services, he welcomed Rianna to the pulpit to introduce the guest preacher, something she insisted on doing.

Stiles shook his head and glanced at Rianna who was seated on the front row directly in front of the pulpit with the biggest smile plastered on her delusional face. *This chick is bat crazy. But enough is enough. No more guest preachers after this one. I'm taking God's pulpit back.*

Rising slowly, First Lady Rianna used the flats of her hands to press down her black fitted dress, and repositioned her matching wide brimmed hat before she strolled toward the pulpit like a supermodel.

Stiles stepped from behind the podium to assist her up the three royal purple carpeted steps.

He waited for her to introduce the speaker, although noticing that different from the other times, he'd actually at least been introduced before services to whomever that might be. He didn't see anyone on the front rows other than the deacons, trustees, and armor bearers.

Rianna stood behind the podium, released her hand from Stiles' hand and smiled at him with a slight nod.

"Thank you, Pastor Graham," she said, almost eloquently.

Stiles took his seat behind her in the pulpit and picked up his Bible, while he anticipated who the speaker of the day was going to be.

When Rianna revealed her bedazzled iPhone and thereafter began reading a passage of scripture from it, Stiles almost choked. *What is she doing?*

"Ecclesiastes chapter five, verse eighteen says, and I'm reading from the Easy to Read or ERV version of the Bible," Rianna articulated. "I have seen what is best for people to do on earth. They should eat, drink, and enjoy the work they have during their short time here. God has given them these few days, and that is all they have—Amen." Raising her head, she looked out into the packed congregation.

With a polished lipstick smile, she continued, speaking deliberately. "I'm sure some of you are probably wondering why I'm standing here. You're used to Pastor Graham or a guest preacher delivering God's Word. But God is in control and I have to be obedient to his direction." She briefly glanced over her shoulder at Stiles who still wore a confused look. "Many of you know that my husband, the senior pastor of this great church, New Holy Rock, is incarcerated. Yes, he may be a man of God, but he has to suffer the consequences of his own mistakes and choices. Well, I'm standing here on his behalf. God has been dealing with me for some time now about the ministry. I don't know if you are aware that my husband had a heart attack a few weeks ago. Thank God he's going to be okay. It's what prompted me to move forward with what the Lord has been calling me to do."

Some of the congregation clapped and others could be heard saying, "Amen" and "Praise God."

Rianna continued babbling while Stiles grew more uncomfortable with each word she spoke. She started ranting and raving about how God wants everyone to enjoy life, have fun, don't take life too seriously, party a little, live it up a lot, and in essence she promoted self-indulgence.

At the end of her fifteen minutes she closed with, "When you leave here today, go enjoy yourselves. Spend a little money. Ladies, use those credit cards tucked away in your husband's wallets." She chuckled loudly. Tapping her flat hand on the pulpit she continued. "Eat, drink, and yes, be merry! Live life to the fullest. Stop being a bunch of stuck up religious folks. Live. Can I get an Amen." She twirled around, clapped her hands, and broke out in song.

There were a couple of soft hand claps but the majority of the congregation remained quiet as they gawked at the woman who now proclaimed to be a messenger of God.

Stiles couldn't wait for her to end her song. He rose from his seat and sprinted up next to her.

"Thank you, First Lady McCoy for that uh untraditional message. Amen." Stiles stuttered followed with a light hand clap.

A few members clapped too and swiftly Stiles opened the doors of the church. It was no surprise when no one came forward.

Rianna remained at the front of the sanctuary so members could come and greet her at the end of service. Several did come forward, shook her hand, and congratulated her. This only seemed to inflate Rianna's ego, because she smiled and threw her headful of fresh blonde weave over her shoulders.

After everyone was gone, Stiles tried pulling her to the side. "Let me talk to you for a minute, Sista Rianna."

"I'm sorry, we'll have to do it another time. I'm headed to brunch and my friend is waiting on me." She looked at Tiny who was standing toward the back of the church near the exit.

Stiles was clearly agitated, shook his head, and walked off leaving a smiling Rianna to go to the back where Tiny waited.

"How'd I do?" she asked when she and Tiny walked outside the church.

"It was different is all I can say. I like the part about living life to the fullest and having fun. I don't know how some of the other folks took it, and I don't know much about what the Bible says, but it was on point for me."

They high-fived and trotted to their respective cars. "I'll meet you at Memphis Barbeque."

"Okay, I have to stop for gas and then I'm headed there," Tiny said and the ladies got inside their cars.

Tiny laughed to herself when she thought about how bold and fierce Rianna was. The girl didn't let nothing or nobody keep her from doing whatever she wanted.

†

Hezekiah was pleased with his return to Sunday service. He preached about forgiveness and redemption. He had a small praise team who song their hearts out. He noticed there were quite a few new inmates in attendance in the open space where he held the services. Rows of steel chairs were lined up and almost every one of them was filled. At the end of the hour and half long service, four inmates came forward asking for more information about giving their lives to Christ.

Later that afternoon, he called his brother from the prison phone system.

"I'm glad to hear your first Sunday back was a good one. I told you, God has you covered, brother," Stiles reassured him. "I wish I could say the same for your wife."

When Stiles told Hezekiah about Rianna's latest antics, Hezekiah almost blew a gasket.

"I can't believe her. Dang, she's mocking God now? And you let her? Man, you should have got up and told her to sit her behind down."

"You know I couldn't do that, but I'm going to talk to her. I tried to after service ended but she brushed me off. Said someone was waiting on her."

"You can't let that happen again. Man, I'm so sick of her. She's spending all my money, living in my house, and now she wants to mock God, pretending like she was called to preach—because of me. Are you kidding me?"

"Look, I didn't want to get you upset. You need to chill. You're just gaining back your strength. Don't let Rianna get you riled up. The devil will use any tactics he can to get you off course, but remember, you have bigger fish to fry. We need to get you out of there."

"Yeah, tell me about it. "

"Did Trevor Price come see you? He said he was driving up there a couple days ago."

"Yeah, he came. Seems to know his stuff, at least when it comes to divorce."

"That's his specialty. You know he's the same lawyer that was representing Xavier. That is until Xavier and Pepper thankfully decided to give their marriage another go."

"Yeah, I know." Hezekiah continued sweating and clearing his throat. "He brought the papers. I signed them and he's going to file. It's all in the works. Everything should be in order in the next few weeks. I bet I hear from her when she finds out she no longer has access to my money. Not even the money she was getting from New Holy Rock. Oh, and I want her fired from her Minister of Music duties."

"Are you sure about that?"

"Heck, yeah. I'm a hundred percent sure. Also, when I talked to him about the divorce that meant talking about my finances. I told him as fast as money comes in Rianna gobbles it up. He offered a solution to that too."

"What'd he say? Dude is a shark when it comes to getting everything to work in his client's favor."

"He explained the importance of having a Power of Attorney while I'm in here. I always thought it was for folks on the verge of dementia or who could no longer take care of themselves or make competent decisions. Long story short, after he explained how it could protect me, I made him my Power of Attorney or as some call it, POA."

"Okay. You sure you're good with that?" asked Stiles.

"Yes, I'm actually relieved. It takes a lot of stress off of me while I'm trying to do this time. Do you know anything about a POA?"

"Yeah, only because of Pastor. Josie is his POA. What about your credit cards? Can he stop her from using them?"

"He could have but he told me how to handle that. I was able to get a hold of the credit card companies from my cell last night and got them suspended. It was easier than I thought since they were in my name. I was told any charges from this point forward that she tries to make will be denied. You *did* talk to the church board about changing the accounts? Right?"

"Yes, we met this past Tuesday. Xavier was present and Attorney Price came. He explained that he represented you. He told them of your concerns in regard to the first lady, what he proposed to do about those concerns, and at the end he answered any questions they had, which there were few. The meeting went smoothly. Rest assured everything is being taken care of. And before you say it, yes I did tell Sista Rianna about the meeting, because according to protocol, I had to—she sits on the board. As usual she didn't bother to show up. Of course, I may have forgotten to mention the nature of the meeting." Stiles chuckled over the phone line.

"I bet you did," Hezekiah laughed.

"I was banking on her not showing up and she did not disappoint," Stiles said. "You had a couple of trustees who were on Rianna's side, but in the end they saw the truth for what it was. Xavier found some discrepancies that he presented as well. Basically, showed she was robbing you blind. The majority voted, and First Lady Rianna McCoy will not receive another dime of the salary you get from New Holy Rock. Now that Trevor is working on the POA, your finances should be back under your control in no time at all. If she's to get anything, it will be decided by the court."

Hezekiah chuckled, placed a hand over his chest, and started coughing again. "Yep, and now that I know he's filing the divorce papers all is well, brother." He cleared his throat. "All's well. I've been handling my affairs as best I can since I've been in here, especially since she's shown me her true colors. Behind bars or not, she's going to learn not to mess with Hezekiah McCoy."

fourteen

"Camouflage is a game we all like to play, but our secrets are as surely revealed by what we want to seem to be as by what we want to conceal." R. Lynes

Hezekiah felt more energized with each passing day. His depression was gone and he was twenty-something pounds lighter. At his last infirmary visit, the nurse told him his heart was working perfectly.

Today he had a meeting with his criminal defense attorney. The same one who was working on an appeal and trying to find a loophole, any loophole, to get him released.

A guard appeared, had him turn backwards in his cell, back up to the door, and put his hands behind his back. The guard proceeded to handcuff him before unlocking the heavy steel door.

Next, he ushered Hezekiah into a dark, dank, private visiting area reserved where inmates could talk confidently with their lawyers.

"How are you today?" the lawyer asked when Hezekiah came in and took a seat.

"Better every day. God is good. I hope to be even better if you got something good to tell me."

"I do have some good news with a little not so good news mixed in. What do you want to hear first?"

Hezekiah shrugged. "Good? Bad? Don't matter. I got to hear it all one way or the other."

"Good news is the DA made an arrest."

"An arrest? When? Who?"

"Yesterday. They arrested a suspect believed to be responsible for shooting you."

Hezekiah slammed his palm down on the gray steel table and his eyes stretched wide open like somebody who had thyroid issues. "Are you serious? I didn't think they were doing much on it since I'm locked up. They don't give two nickels about a free Black man being victimized so you know what they think about me being up in here. The case went cold, or so I thought. Who was it?" Hezekiah inquired; his voice anxious and quick. "Who wanted me dead?"

"You're right, the case had gone cold, but from what I learned they got a tip. Out of the blue. And guess who the caller named as your shooter?"

Hezekiah squinted and leaned in slightly on the table. "Who? Who is it?"

"Your son's father or I should say *stepfather.*"

"Mariah's husband? You can't be serious." Hezekiah paused in thought. "Then again, it does make sense. Well I'll be..." Hezekiah cussed. "He *was* highly upset when he thought I could have been the one responsible for his incredulous past being revealed. Then me gaining custody of Jude, even if it was for a short time, made him even angrier. I think he may have even lost his job after that. What do I care now that I know he's the one who tried to take me out?"

"Remember you said that the shooter was upset because you had ruined things with his family," the lawyer reminded.

"Yeah, right, right. That's what he was saying. Did they get him to confess? How did it go down?"

"The tipster actually had evidence on her cell phone between her, and yes I said, *her*—

Hezekiah balled up a fist and put it to his mouth and then erupted in laughter. "Her? Dude was cheating on Mariah *and* he's a pedophile? Go figure."

"Yeah, go figure. Well, the conversation between them, he told her things were rocky in his marriage and that it was mainly because of you, his stepson's daddy. He told her you were putting your nose into business that wasn't yours. That you didn't have a relationship with Jude and you didn't want him and Jude to have one either. There you go."

"Motive," Hezekiah, said, shaking his head and placing both hands flat on the table. "Now that I think about what he said, yeah, he sounded furious."

"Furious enough to want to kill you. After bringing him in without incident, he basically confessed after we told him what we had on him."

"Man, that's good news. Nah, that's great news," Hezekiah shouted and roared with laughter.

"Now for the not so good news—I'm stepping down as your lawyer."

"You're what? Why? I need you, man. You're the best criminal defense lawyer in this city. What's going on?" Hezekiah's voice was stern and serious. His brows furrowed as he bit down on his bottom lip.

"I'm not just stepping down from *you*; I'm leaving the firm altogether. I'm not well."

"Not well? What do you mean?"

"I was," the lawyer hesitated, "I was given a year, maybe two...left to live."

Hezekiah's mean glare turned to one of sympathy as his face took on a relaxed but serious expression. "Nah, say it isn't so. What's wrong?"

"It's Lou Gehrig's or as most folks call it, ALS. I've been having symptoms that I attributed to all the long hours I work. You know always on the run while trying to successfully juggle family life. So I didn't think much of anything when I started feeling weak in my muscles. But lately, when I started tripping, falling a lot, dropping things, I knew something wasn't right. Then when I started finding it hard to argue my cases, especially as of late, my wife insisted I see a doctor. I listened, went to my doctor who sent me to a neurologist. They did a battery of tests and bingo—ALS," he said with sarcasm. "The average life expectancy is two to five years from the time of diagnosis. I don't want to spend that time representing clients. I want to be with my family, around my family, enjoy them as much as I can for however long I can."

"Man, I'm sorry to hear that." Hezekiah rested his head in his hands and shook his head. Looking up, he said, "God has the final say. Look at me," he joked and tried to chuckle but couldn't. "I've defied the odds at least three times!"

The lawyer laughed. "Really, I'm not worried. Whatever hand life deals me I'm rolling with it. As for my clients, I'm turning over all my cases, including yours, to this new attorney who recently joined the firm. He's supposed to be a tycoon when it comes to criminal defense. He's thirty-five years old, been in practice going on ten years, half that time as a lead criminal defense attorney who's won ninety-eight and a half percent of his cases. Don't ask me about the half." The lawyer chuckled. "Hails from the Big Apple by way of the Windy City. Especially well known in Harlem, Manhattan, Jersey, New York City, you can just say basically all over the Big Apple. Highly successful and respected by his colleagues."

"Answer me this."

"Sure," said the lawyer.

"If he was held at such high regard in New York what brings him to the South? Especially to Memphis? Never mind, let me answer that. Is it the fact Memphis is the number one murder capital in the country, and he sees lots of dollar signs?" Hezekiah mocked.

"Let me just say the benefits package the firm offered him is nothing to sneeze at, that's for sure. Combined with the low cost of living here and that makes that seven figure salary plus perks even more attractive—not to mention lucrative. The man can easily live like a multi-millionaire in this town. But his official reason? His wife is an executive for that new pharmaceutical company chain whose southern headquarters opened downtown a few months back. She's their Executive Vice-President, Pharmaceutical Sales. They're relocating her from their New York office to Memphis. You know she's bringing in the big bucks too, so I guess he's doing like any good spouse, he's following her. From what I was told during our morning briefing he's still going to maintain an affiliation with the New York firm, at least for the next eighteen months, but we're bringing him on as partner and the new lead criminal defense attorney. It couldn't be better timing with me resigning."

Hezekiah remained quiet. The only sign that he heard any of what his lawyer said was the slight nod he gave.

"You have nothing to worry about. You'll be in more than capable hands. You should be hearing from him in the next few weeks. They're still in the process of relocating and he's going over my main cases, which includes yours of course. I think you'll like him."

Hezekiah spoke up, deliberately. "What's his name?"

"Christianaldo William Black. He goes by "Christian Black."

"Interesting, well let's see if this Christianaldo fellow can produce some miracles. With a name like that, let's pray that he can and that he will," Hezekiah said, almost jokingly.

"Who knows, with fresh eyes on your case, and somebody like Black working on it, things can take a change for the better. You just have to stay hopeful. Don't give up."

"Gotcha," said Hezekiah. "I hope everything goes well with you too, man. It's got to be a hard battle for you and your family, but with God on your side you can conquer anything. I have much love and respect for you. You've been with me a long time. I appreciate you being my lawyer and someone I consider a friend."

The lawyer stood, walked around to where Hezekiah was starting to rise, and the two men embraced.

"Take care of yourself," the teary-eyed lawyer said as he called for the guard to let him out of the room.

"You do the same. God bless ya," Hezekiah said as the guard appeared and led him up the hall back toward his pod.

fifteen

"You walked into my life like you had always lived there, like my heart was a home built just for you." Unknown

"Honey, I think that was the last of the boxes. The movers will be back in the morning to finish unpacking and putting everything in its proper place. That's going to be a big relief. I couldn't see myself unpacking another single thing. How did we ever live without hired help?"

Christian looked at his wife and laughed. "You are truly one of a kind."

"I know, and you better not ever forget it." She sashayed up next to him. Standing on her tip toes she still didn't reach his lips, but he leaned down to meet hers.

His soft thick lips devoured her thin polished lips. His smooth as a baby's bottom hands gently but firmly caressed the contours of her thickness, traveling over the large curve of her rear. He was always easily pulled into her beauty. After eleven years together, nine of those years as a married couple, Christian considered himself a blessed man.

A native of Bluffton, one of the richest cities in South Carolina, thirty-eight year old Luna Grace Newsom was a virgin when she met Christianaldo at the start of both their careers. They quickly fell in love. She had graduated with a doctorate in pharmaceutical and went on to garner a lucrative position at a global pharmaceutical company in pharmaceutical sales.

Christianaldo, from Chicago and three years Luna's junior, had recently passed the bar with flying colors, and had been hired full time by the law firm in New York where he had interned and worked as a law clerk while attending the prestigious private New York University School of Law.

The childless couple met at a downtown Starbucks in Manhattan. He was on his way to his first deposition and she was on her way to make a pharmaceutical sales call. They both stopped in Starbucks on an otherwise typical routine rainy day in New York. She had ordered and received her favorite frappe, turned around, but like the age old tale, bumped into Christianaldo, almost ruining his stylish tailored three piece suit, had he not quickly stepped back in the nick of time.

From that initial encounter, the two became inseparable. Both learned later they were raised in church and she, more so than

Christian, was fiercely religious. It was Luna who helped him learn the importance of forgiving others, especially his mother who died six weeks after Christian and Luna met.

Within weeks of their relationship approaching the two year mark, Christian proposed and Luna readily accepted. He felt secure in his new position as a lawyer and she felt exceptionally good about her career in pharmaceutical sales so they ventured into living life together. They had been flying high ever since.

The move to Memphis was one they both talked about in great detail. They had already made conscientious efforts to always support each other. This time was no different. Christianaldo would follow her to the ends of the earth and she would do the same for him.

After hours of doing some unpacking of their own, the exhausted couple lay in their king bed.

"Thank God we got the movers to put our bed up. Everything else can wait, but I was not looking forward to spending another night at a hotel."

Christian turned over on his side and pulled his wife underneath his arm. Kissing her on top of her forehead, he began caressing her, taking satisfaction in hearing her familiar love sounds. It was his sign that she was ready and willing for him to make love to her, something she never denied him.

As much as he loved her, he had not always been faithful, something he was not proud of. If she ever found out that he had a one night stand with a former colleague, it would destroy her. It happened years ago, not long after they got married. Like most affairs, it started with a mutual attraction and then at a gathering one evening, one where his wife was unable to attend, he committed the act of adultery after having far too much alcohol.

It was unbridled sex of which afterwards they quickly apologized to each other, vowing never to speak of it again. A year or so later, his colleague left the firm after relocating to another state. Christian made a promise to God that he would walk the straight and narrow and never ever cheat on his wife again. He had kept that promise.

Hours later, Christian and Luna woke up in each other's arms. "We have to find a church," Luna whispered, not wanting to move from the warmth of her husband's massive arms that clutched her like a teddy bear.

He kissed her again. "Find a church. Is that what you're thinking about after we just had wild crazy sex?" he said, smiling big.

She looked up at him and smiled too. "No, it's not that. It just went through my mind.

You know how I feel about being part of a congregation. It makes me feel complete. To start the week off on a Sunday by going to church and fellowshipping with others just makes the week better."

"Yeah, I know. I have a couple of places that was suggested by some of the firm," Christian said.

"Me too. A couple of co-workers told me about the church they attend. One name that keeps popping up is a church called New Holy Rock."

Christian eased up and sat in the bed, his back resting against the oversized solid wood headboard. "That's funny. One of the lawyers suggested Holy Rock Ministries in a subdivision I think he called *Whitehaven*. I wonder if it's the same church."

Luna sat up in the bed too. "I don't know; maybe. I just want a church where both of us can feel like we belong. It needs to be diverse. I don't want to be the only biracial chick, and I surely don't want to be a dumpy short fat one at that," she went on describing herself.

Christian looked at his wife, smiled and grabbed her. "I guess that makes you my fat, short, mixed chick who I happen to love," Christian said, squeezing his wife's robust pillowy body. "I love every single chunky chunk chunk of you. Arrrh, arrrh," he said, taking fake bites of her while kissing her all over her face to her mounds.

Luna laughed, picked up one of the bed pillows and threw it at him. "You are *sooo* wrong for that," she said, laughing then kissing him back.

"Seriously though, I told you I don't like it when you talk down about yourself. I love you and you should love you too—just the way you are. If you aren't happy with yourself, you alone have the power to change, but don't change for me or anyone else, because sweetheart, I love you for you. You're the same person I met in Starbucks on that stormy day. You brought a ray of sunshine in my life that has never gone away," he said, kissing her again.

Squeezing her tighter, he said, "Luna, honey, I know you. You want us to find a church like the one we came from in New York. Where everyone was accepted as one big congregation, where everyone had one focus—to worship God, no judgment."

"Right, and to be honest that's one thing that made me a little hesitant about relocating to Memphis. I've heard the South can be a big culture shock for folks like us who are used to the Northeast way of living."

"I think you're panicking for nothing. I don't think we'll have a problem finding the perfect church. We're in the Bible belt, after all. There's a church on just about every corner. Honestly, I've never seen anything like it," Christian said, shaking his head and laughing. "Think about it, I don't know about you, but like I told you at least three or four members of my law firm have told me about a dozen or more churches in all areas of the city."

"Same with me. It's just that I miss our church family so much. And not being in church on Sundays feels funny," she lamented. "They say racism and prejudice reeks in the South, especially here in Memphis. It's bad to say, but I'm scared for you, baby, you know you being a Black man. I don't know why I accepted this move. I should have thought about this more, should have thought more about how it would affect you."

"*Shhh*," Christian whispered, kissing her on top of her hair. "You did. We did. So please, stop." He continued light kisses on top of her hair and stroking the side of her face. "Your faith is stronger than this. We both talked about this and prayed about it, baby. In the end, we believed and agreed God wanted you and me to be here. Look how doors opened, and I mean opened wide for me with Brachman Law Firm. It's the top law firm in Memphis and I'm going to be a partner. A partner, Luna. Look at yourself. You're a freaking Executive

Vice President for one of the largest pharmaceutical companies in the country! We're doing extremely well financially. Baby, this move is already proving to be a blessing. Trust me, this move is ordained by God."

Luna eased up in the bed next to her husband. "I love you, I trust you, and I trust God."

"You watch what I tell you, we're going to find the perfect church," Christian reassured his wife.

"Yes, I know, and it's going to be a church where not only we are loved and welcomed but a church where our children, if or when we ever decide to adopt," she said, briefly pausing and looking at Christian, "will be accepted no matter what race they are. That's something I think we both agree on."

"Yes, of course."

Luna reached for and grabbed her phone from off the nightstand table next to their bed. "I'm going to look up some of the churches. Maybe we can start visiting this Sunday."

"Sounds good," Christian readily agreed.

Scrolling, Luna googled New Holy Rock. Right away the location and an image of the church appeared. Next she put in Holy Rock Ministries, and another image, different from New Holy Rock, appeared."

"Honey, they aren't the same; they're two different churches. See," she said, showing him her phone while using her free hand to sling back her flowing red curly hair. "From these pictures, it looks like a diverse group. Mostly Black but I do see some Whites and Latinos. We can visit around. I'm sure we'll find something."

"Yeah, look at this. Looks like this may be a family, brothers or something 'cause look right there," Christian pointed, "both of the pastors share the same last name—McCoy, and the churches have similar names too," said Christian, looking surprised as if he'd just received a revelation. Perhaps he had.

sixteen

"Perhaps one did not want to be loved so much as to be understood." G. Orwell

Sista Mavis paraded around Holy Rock like she was the official First Lady. Her silver mane had grown, reaching to the center of her back. She professed to never having put even the slightest bit of perm in it—ever. She usually wore it naturally curly and fluffy or straight pressed in a ponytail that flowed down the middle of her back like she wore it today.

Anything about anything and anybody that had to do with Holy Rock you could count on Sista Mavis knowing something about it. All in all the sixty-eight year old woman was a force to be reckoned with, and could quote scripture with the best of them. She held up the front office, and now that Eliana was First Lady Sista Mavis had moved up to the pastor and the First Lady's assistant. She thought she was hot stuff when she was given that role that came with a big salary increase. Couldn't tell her nothing. She was spry for her age but the position didn't require a lot of anything stressful for the woman who was young at heart and loved herself some Pastor Khalil. He was like the son she never had.

"Hey, Pastor K," she said before the start of mid-week Bible service. "Did you and First Lady get your dinner?"

Khalil approached Sista Mavis, kissed her on the cheek, and gave her a squeeze around her thick waist.

"Yes, Sista Mavis, we just finished," he said, looking over at Eliana when she approached holding their daughter.

The little girl instantly reached for her doting father who proudly accepted her and kissed his little princess.

Sista Mavis leaned over and hugged Eliana. "She is such a doll, a precious treasure from heaven. The two of you are so blessed. Isn't that right, First Lady?"

"Yes, we are. God is so good, Sista Mavis. Speaking of dinner, it was perfect. The Kitchen Ministry gets better every week. Lots of fresh veggies, salads, and fruit. I love how they incorporate plant-based cooking into the menu, too. It makes for a healthier eating congregation. Changing the menu up was a good suggestion Sista Campbell made."

"Yes, that woman is remarkable. A young thang too. Can't be no older than you and Pastor K," Sista Mavis said, smiling with approval. "Do you need me to watch this precious little one so you can enjoy midweek service?" Sista Mavis gently pinched the baby's rosy cheek and made a kissy face.

"That won't be necessary, Sista Mavis, but what about if you sit with us. That way if she *does* start fussing, maybe you—I mean, uh."

"Stop, I would love to. I was on my way to close down everything in the office and lock up for the evening. I'll meet you in the sanctuary in just a minute."

"Okay, thanks Sista Mavis."

†

On the other end of the city, Xavier and Pepper unloaded the boys from their car seats and trudged inside the house. It had been a long, tiring day. Working at New Holy Rock all day and then staying over for midweek Bible study, could be taxing. There was always somebody pulling at him, calling him, needing him to look up this report, or run that report, or help with this and that. Not to mention his responsibilities working in the Youth Ministry. It seemed endless. Added to having to juggle a family, sometimes Xavier felt quite overwhelmed. He was glad to finally be at home and settled in with his wife and kids.

Xavier and his family by outside appearances were the perfect happy family.

Yet, deep inside Xavier was more miserable than ever. His demons were constantly at war with his mind and flesh. Although he hadn't stepped outside of his marriage anymore, he still had the underlying urge and desire to do so. He prayed every day for strength to maintain his devotion to Pepper and the boys.

After returning home from Bible study, the couple got the boys ready for bed before the couple relaxed in their family room.

"How was your day?" Pepper asked, munching on a bowl of hot buttered popcorn while snuggling up against her husband. Going from one TV channel to the next, she stopped on a show she thought would hold both of their interests.

Xavier inhaled and then released a long slow breath. "It was okay. Another day of shuffling files, making calls, etcetera, etcetera. That's it. The same old routine," he said somberly, barely looking at his wife. "Even going to church two and three times a week for this type of service and that type of meeting; it's exhausting. I love God and I love the ministry, but it's becoming, I don't know," Xavier paused as if struggling to find what words to say next, "I'm just not feeling it like I used to. To be honest, I haven't been feeling it for a long, long time, Pepper."

"If you're unhappy, why don't you find something else? I mean you do have your Bachelor's in Finance. You can go other places. You could even go into corporate America if you wanted to. You're not stuck working for your daddy and uncle or for a church, honey. You could even work for yourself."

Xavier still didn't make eye contact but spoke while looking aimlessly ahead. He shrugged, "I don't know. I'm just not feeling fulfilled anymore. I...don't want to sound ungrateful because I know we have a good life. I make good money. I'm able to provide well for you and the boys. You don't have to work, unless you want to. I mean, everything from the outside looks good. It's just that—"

"It doesn't give you the satisfaction you're looking for. It's not your passion .I understand."

This time he did turn his head and look at his wife who was leaning against his shoulder.

"You always know the right thing to say. That's one of the things I love about you, Pepper."

"It's the truth; it's just not something I said to be nice."

Pepper sat upright, placed the bowl of popcorn on the table in front of them, and met her husband's stare. "That's nice of you to say." She almost choked up while she fought back tears that tried to form. Hearing Xavier say he loved her in any form was special. She loved him and she wanted so badly for their marriage to work. They didn't talk openly about it too often, but Pepper believed her husband was doing all he could to keep his family together. She couldn't imagine the torment he was going through wrestling with his feelings. Every day she prayed for him to find peace in living a heterosexual lifestyle.

"Ever since we first met, I found it easy to talk to you. That's why we hit it off from the beginning." Xavier released a smile at the thought. "You're such a good listener. Another thing I especially admire about you is you listen without judgment. I know this has to be tough for you. Knowing your husband desires men?" He looked even deeper into her eyes and wrapped an arm around her shoulder. "You're a good woman. I don't deserve you. I want you to know that I'm working on myself every day, Pepper— I promise I am. I want to be the best husband and the best father. I want us to have the best marriage without all these crazy thoughts racing through my head." This time Xavier fought back tears, but he was unsuccessful. They flowed silently down his face.

Pepper reached up and gently wiped them away while kissing his lips and telling him between kisses, "I love you, Xavier McCoy. I want to make you happy. I won't ever judge you. I promise I won't. We can do this, babe. I know we can. We can make this work—together."

"I love you, too, Pepper. I do."

Xavier leaned in and Pepper met his lips with hers.

When their lips parted, Xavier exhaled again. "You're right. Maybe it's time I look at new career opportunities. I'm tired of doing what everybody else expects me to do. I want to live my own life."

"If that means stepping away from ministry work and finding something outside the church, I say go for it. I'm going to support you in whatever you decide. You got me. I'm not going anywhere," Pepper reassured her husband.

The couple kissed again, only this time, their passion was unstoppable, raw, heated, and before you know it, they were making love on the sofa as visions of *Ian* danced in Xavier's head.

seventeen

"Facts do not cease to exist because they are ignored." Aldous Huxley

Rianna was growing more impatient with Abel. It had been over two and half months and he still had not returned to Memphis. If he had, he sure as heck didn't tell her. He barely, if ever, called her now, and when they did talk, it was short and abrupt. Totally unlike Big Daddy.

She facetimed him today while sitting in her living room inside Apartment 3D. Expecting the call to go to voicemail, she was surprised when his face appeared on the screen.

"Big Daddy, omg, I'm so glad I got you. What's going on? I miss you? When are you coming back?" she asked, looking almost frantic while talking rapidly like she had to get in every word quickly before he hung up.

"Look, bae, I've been meaning to call, but things have been hectic. I'm actually glad you called because I need to tell you something."

Her heart started racing and she braced herself for what she could only think had to be bad news.

"Okay," she said, cautiously. "What is it?"

"I'm not coming back. I sold my tire company and I'm going to stay in Seattle. I've got some new and better business ventures taking off here." His expression was serious; veins appeared on the side of his temples.

"You're what?" Rianna's breath was cut short. She couldn't believe what she was hearing. She pounced up off the couch and quickly started pacing. "What are you talking about, Abel? What do you mean you're not coming back?" she screamed into the phone, spit flying out of her mouth. "And when did you sale your business? You worked that business from the ground up to make it what it is today. Tell me what's really going on, Abel?"

"Look, I can't go into detail. All you need to know is some things came up making it impossible for me to leave anytime soon. My partner in the Memphis company bought me out. As for my business here, things are great. Better than great, actually. But enough of me, how are you, my love?" he asked, suddenly smiling on the screen while he took a drag off his cigarette.

"Don't you *how are you my love* me, Abel Cane. How can you do this? And how long have you known you weren't coming back?" she asked, her anger quickly rising to surface. "I don't understand. Do you, do you want me to come there? If that's the case, you know I can't do that right now. I have to wait until I can clear things up with Hezekiah. I need you to make sense, Big Daddy."

"Look, chill out. That's all I can tell you. Just know I won't be back, not anytime soon." More frown lines appeared on his otherwise olive skinned face. "It's over Rianna. I have to admit, it was good while it lasted, but it's time you and I both move on. I have a wife and you have a husband. It is what it is."

"I...I don't know what to say. Look, why don't I fly up there this weekend, or if that won't work, I can take a flight out tomorrow or Thursday, spend a day or two and we can talk about this. I miss you, Big Daddy. You can't let things end like this. I know you don't mean it," she said, pleading as her face turned crimson and tears appeared.

"I do mean it and no, I don't want you flying up here. That won't change anything. And save your tears, sweetheart. Remember, I know how you can turn them on and off like a faucet at will. You and me have always known this wasn't a forever thing. Yes, we made a good team. You scratched my back and I scratched yours, but I'm a businessman. You know that. And right now my business is here in Seattle. Look, I have to go, talk to you later, kiddo."

"But, Big—

Abel's face disappeared from the screen and the screen turned blue.

"That low down s-o-b," Rianna sobbed, throwing her phone over on the sofa and storming into her galley kitchen. She retrieved a bottle of wine from the bottom cabinet and then stormed back to the living room, opened the wine bottle, and turned it up to her lips.

"I don't need you, Abel! I don't need you, Hezekiah! I don't need nobody," she ranted and took another big gulp of the white wine. "That's why I don't trust nobody. Folks will always find a way to screw you. Well, forget you Big Daddy. Forget you all. Rianna Jamison McCoy don't need nobody," she said, sobbing. "Nobody."

†

The following week was rainy, overcast most days, and rather dreary. The summer breeze mixed with the incoming fall of the year made things even nastier. It was like Mother Nature was bipolar with all the fluctuating temps and weather patterns.

The ugly weather matched Rianna's mood. Ever since Big Daddy broke things off, she was in a funk. She became even more upset when she saw she couldn't pull up his social media accounts. He did a lot of social media interactions for his business, and she was no longer able to access any of his sites. Had he blocked her?

She hadn't left out of Apartment 3D since Abel's call. Tiny had been calling, texting, and facetiming her, but she ignored her. She wasn't in the mood or frame of mind to hear Tiny's hood chick advice. Not today, not tomorrow. Maybe never.

The knock on the door of Apartment 3D startled her. "Who the heck can this be?" she asked herself. She glanced at the stylish wall clock. It wasn't quite noon. She ignored the knock but when it continued and grew louder she casually strolled to the door, peeped through the peephole and saw Tiny's petite self standing on the other side.

"I know you're in there, trick," Tiny yelled and started pounding on the door again. "Open this dang door. I'm not leaving 'til you do." She pounded again.

Rianna unlatched the door and turned the knob. Slowly, she opened the door and stepped aside.

Tiny boldly entered, slamming the door closed behind her. "What in the heck is wrong with you? You look like death two times over," she remarked.

Rianna strolled off and then plopped down on the sofa. "Abel broke things off with me. I don't understand. What's going on, Tiny? Lately, it seems like my life is falling apart."

"Look, you and I both know Big Daddy was just a past time. You did for him and he did for you. Not once have I ever heard you say you loved him or that he loved you. You know for yourself it wasn't going to last forever. You got what you got out of him and now that train has run its course. Let it go. You're better than this. The Rianna I know would never let a man, especially one who you didn't love, get in between the way of her dreams or living her life."

Rianna looked over at Tiny who had sat down in the recliner across from the sofa. Tiny got up, went over and sat next to Rianna. She hugged her friend. "It's gon' be all right. Everything's gonna work out just the way it's s'posed to."

Rianna eased out of her friend's embrace and looked at her while she wiped away her tears. "You're right, Tiny. What was I thinking? I'm not going to let Big Daddy or any man or any person for that matter make me go to a dark place. I've got too much going on."

"That's my girl," Tiny said, patting her shoulder and smiling. "It's Friday, I just got paid *and* my child tax credit money just posted to my account. Let me treat you to lunch. We can splurge a little. But still nothing too expensive," she mocked. "I don't have deep pockets like you, girlfriend," Tiny teased.

"I tell you what, you buy lunch and I'll treat you to a couple of new outfits to seduce your baby daddy. That'll be some good retail therapy." They both started laughing.

"Spending Hezekiah's coins always makes me forget all about these
momentary troubles. Whaddaya say, Tiny?"

"I say, let's go live it up by spending it up!"

The friends dined at a popular seafood restaurant out East and then headed to their favorite shopping mall.

In and out of store after store, the ladies window shopped. After several hours of looking at one outfit after another, they lingered in Nordstrom's. Both ladies found several outfits they liked.

"Make sure you pick out shoes and accessories to match," Rianna urged Tiny.

"Are you sure?" Tiny asked, looking at Rianna like she wasn't sure about this whole thing. "I don't want you to think I'm taking advantage of you."

"Girl, please. You don't even know what the word advantage means. Get what you want. We only live once. Go on now."

"I think I'm going to get this one and this one," Rianna said, holding up a jumpsuit and a gorgeous Fendi dress.

"I love both of them," Tiny replied. "Look at this. She showed Rianna a fancy teal pantsuit and a pair of sparkly colorful shoes to match.

"Is that it? Is that all you want?" Rianna asked, eyeing the outfit and shoes. "I love it, but if you want something else, go for it. I may not feel like being this generous tomorrow," Rianna bellowed.

"I'm good. All I need to do is find me a necklace and some earrings. Maybe a small purse."

"Okay, take your time. I'm going to the fragrance section."

"Okay," Tiny said, and they sprinted in opposite directions.

Twenty five minutes later they met up at the front of the store at the register. Piling their stash on top of the counter, Rianna eagerly pulled out her credit card. "Here you go," she said to the retail clerk.

"Thank you, but all you have to do is insert your card right there," the clerk said and pointed to the credit card machine on the counter.

"Oops, that's right." Rianna inserted the card, waited for a few seconds and it came back TRY ANOTHER FORM OF PAYMENT.

"Ma'am, that card was declined. Do you have another form of payment? Perhaps another credit card? Cash?"

"No, let me try it again," she insisted. "There must be something wrong with this darn machine," she barked, flustered when for a second time the card was declined.

"Oh, well, here use this one." She retrieved her Black card from her wallet and inserted it. The same words appeared on the screen.

The clerk rolled her eyes up in head. "Ma'am."

"Ma'am nothing. There's something wrong with your machine. My cards have never been declined," Rianna said, her voice elevating.

Tiny tugged lightly on her friend's jacket sleeve. "Don't worry about it," she whispered. "It's probably a glitch somewhere. You know how these machines can be. Come on, we can come back tomorrow."

"No, Tiny, there's nothing wrong with my cards." Frantically, Rianna put those cards back inside her wallet and then pulled out her debit card. "Let me use this. I know this one better work," she fussed. "I have plenty of funds to cover this." Sure enough when she inserted her debit card, the $1635.13 charge went through effortlessly.

The clerk gave the ladies their shopping bags full of items and Rianna and Tiny rushed out of the store like they were expecting the woman to call them back inside.

Practically storming out of the mall, Rianna fussed. "I have to call the credit card folks. Something isn't right. Those cards should not be maxed out. I know I've been spending, but I've never not been able to use them."

"Maybe you *have* maxxed them out and didn't know it. You know how you can spend and you don't always think about the amount you spend either," Tiny told her.

"Yeah, that may be true, but I don't have a good feeling about this. I want to try another store."

"Okay, suit yourself," Tiny said.

Rianna stopped at one of the boutiques she liked along the way. The scene repeated itself when she and Tiny went inside and Rianna tried to use her credit cards to pay for a pair of shoes she had her eyes on.

In a huff, she cussed and blamed the cashier for her transaction not going through.

"I swear, if I find my brother-in-law or anybody has cut off my cards, somebody's going to pay, Tiny. Somebody's going to pay big time."

They went back to Rianna's car and got inside. Before Tiny could fully close her door, Rianna had put the car in DRIVE and sped recklessly out of the parking lot.

eighteen

"Manipulation gets people to do something they aren't likely to do if given the opportunity to think." Unknown

Rianna dropped Tiny off at her apartment and headed toward Lion's Gate. Upon arriving at the gate entrance, she spotted a car that looked like Fancy's car stopped in front of her at the gate. The driver was entering the gate access code.

She looked closer. The woman was indeed Fancy. She had the same round shaped head and natural hairstyle as Fancy. "Yep, that's that stuck up, think she so important, heffa," mouthed Rianna spitefully.

The gates slowly opened and Rianna quickly followed the car before the gate could fully close.

Fancy drove along the private streets, making several turns, not bothering to check her rearview mirrors. She made several turns and maneuvers until she turned on her street, continued driving and then pulled into her driveway. She stopped at the edge of the driveway, let down her window, and looked back at Rianna who had momentarily stopped in the middle of the street in front of Fancy's house.

"What do you want? I know you aren't following me. If you are, you better find yourself someone else to play with, li'l girl."

"Last I checked, this is a free street," Rianna said, laughing.

"No, that's where you're wrong. This is a private community. And another thing, you have no reason to stop in the middle of the street in front of my house. If you want a good behind whooping, I can oblige. Other than that, you need to keep on driving."

"Girl, please. Get off your high horse. Your threats don't mean a thing to me. For your information, Miss Lady, this is a private, gated community of which I am a *proud* resident," Rianna mocked, feeling full of herself. She was in a foul mood after her break up with Abel and her disastrous shopping spree. It felt good to poke jabs at Fancy. Especially since this was the first time the ladies had encountered each other inside Lion's Gate in quite some time.

"Honey, please, folks like you don't belong in Lion's Gate. If it wasn't for poor Hezekiah, you would be out of here like yesterday's trash."

Fancy pushed the inside button to let her window back up, pressed the remote control FOB overhead, and waited for her garage door to open.

She took another look at Rianna who started laughing before showing Fancy the *middle* finger and pressing the accelerator, speeding down the otherwise quiet street and disappearing.

"Uhhh, I can't stand that godless, stupid Jezebel," Fancy ranted as she got out of her car and stormed inside the house.

She was greeted by Sebastian who curled up and around her ankles, purring and meowing.

"Hey, my sweet baby," she said lovingly to the cat. She put her purse, keys, and phone on the counter as she walked into the kitchen, and then reached down to scoop up Sebastian who continued purring against her ear.

After giving the handsome brown and black feline several love pats and rubbing him underneath his chin, she put him back on the floor and went to the pantry to get his food.

Her cell phone rang just as she finished refilling his feeder with food and his automatic water bowl with fresh water. The chunky feline ran to his dish and started chumping away.

She smiled when she saw who the caller was. "Well, hello there, stranger."

"Hey, there. What's up with you over there?"

"I should be asking you the same thing. I called and texted you the other day, but you ignored me." She giggled.

"Yeah, sorry, about that. I didn't mean to ignore you, but *man* I've been so busy. Between New Holy Rock and teaching online classes again, it's been hectic. I had to stop and check on you though. You know you're my favorite girl."

Fancy laughed. "Yeah, I bet that's what you tell all of your ex sista-in-laws," she joked.

Stiles laughed. "Guess that's why I only have one, and boy am I glad it's you. Hey, I was wondering since we haven't had a real sit down visit in a minute, what do you say I treat you to dinner this evening? I know it's short notice, but I miss your company, and boy do I have a lot to fill you in on."

"Sounds good, but I'm just getting home. And I'm tired too, plus I just had a run in with that...ugh I hate to even say her name—Rianna."

"What's she up to now?" Stiles spoke up, concern echoing in his tone.

"She's crazy, then again chick ain't that crazy. She knows better. Anyway, nah, she was just being Rianna. You know, classless, ignorant, ghetto Rianna. But what I was saying I've had a long day. I took on a new client. I have to design their kitchen and family room. After I left that appointment I went to Holy Rock. I was there most of the afternoon working with Sista Mavis on that new senior's project. I think I told you about it. Well, that took all day. You already know working next to Sista Mavis is a task in itself. You gotta love her, but she sure can try your nerves. After that, I just wanted to come home, feed Sebastian, and relax."

"Oh, okay, no problem, we can do it another time," Stiles countered.

"Unless you want to pick up something and come over here," she suggested. "I *am* hungry but I was too lazy to stop and get something. I was going to make me a sandwich or salad and that was it."

"Okay, that's cool. I'll stop and pick up something. Anything particular you have a taste for?"

"Not really. Of course, I can always eat something from Imagine Vegan. If you don't want anything from there, you can stop at Lenny's."

"No, Imagine Vegan sounds good. It's been a minute since I went there. Do you think they still have that spinach dip I like?"

"I don't see why they wouldn't. It is one of their regular menu items."

"Okay, I'll go online, check out their menu. You do the same. I'll text you what I want and you can place the order online or call them. Either way, I'm on my way in their direction now. Put it in my name," Stiles reminded her.

"Okay, will do. See you in a few," she said, and they ended the call.

†

Stiles and Fancy gathered in the family room.

"Wow, this food is better than ever." Stiles took a couple of huge bites of his jumbo jerk chicken sandwich complete with all the trimmings. Slathers of juice from the sandwich ran down his hands.

"I see," said Fancy, laughing and wiping her own mouth.

"They're always on point, I'm telling you. Wait until you sink your teeth into this. Here, taste," she said pushing a forkful of pasta toward him.

He opened his mouth, closed his eyes, and savored the pasta. "Man, this is delish."

"Yep," she said and took a forkful for herself. "Now tell me what's going on. How's my ex-husband?"

"He's good. I drove up there a few days ago. He's lost about twenty pounds, looks super healthy. He was in good spirits. Of course, like always, he asked about you."

Fancy blushed and shifted her eyes away from Stiles. At that moment, Sebastian jumped in her lap.

"Still can't believe you went and got yourself a cat." Stiles reached over and gave the cat a tap on its head.

"Yep, I love him. He gives me a sense of comfort. You know sometimes it can be a little lonely up in this house by myself. I was so used to having the boys and my husband around. Then life took a sharp turn and without warning, look at me," she said, looking around her spacious and tastefully decorated home. "An empty nester, divorced first lady, wanna be interior decorator, and miserable," she said, suddenly breaking down in tears. Sebastian jumped off her lap and back down to the floor.

"Let it out," Stiles urged her. "Let it all out." He stood from his chair and went to Fancy. Sitting next to her, he wrapped his arms around her and she relaxed in the curve of his arms and wept.

"Feel better?" Stiles asked after Fancy cried for several minutes.

She nodded.

He got up and went to the other side of the family room and retrieved a box of tissue that was on a table by the bright orange chair that accented the room.

"Here," he said, placing the box in her lap and sitting back down.

"Thanks. I...I didn't mean to break down like that. I'm sorry."

"No need for apologies. We all need a good cry and a shoulder sometimes. You know I care about you," he assured her.

Fancy sat upright. "I know. I care about you too," she said, looking into Stiles' eyes. "You've stuck by me through thick and thin when you didn't have to. You're a really good friend."

"I try," he said. "Hey, ready to dive into dessert?" He rose from the sofa and headed toward the kitchen.

"Sure, I'm ready. I can't wait," Fancy said, rubbing her hands together and releasing a chuckle. She then wiped the last tear and eagerly awaited Stiles to return with chocolate peanut butter cupcakes. On the tray with the cupcakes was a canteen of coffee, sweetener and creamer.

While they drank coffee and divulged in the decadent cupcakes, Stiles continued filling Fancy in on everything that had transpired over the past weeks.

"OMG, I wish I could have been there to see her in that pulpit," Fancy slapped her thighs and laughed loudly. "Was she honestly preaching and you didn't stream it?"

"It took everything in me not to jump up and snatch that mic out of her hand. Hezekiah knows he picked himself a nut. And you know I wasn't about to stream that. God worked it out because of all Sundays my media guy wasn't at service. Can you believe that?" Stiles laughed.

Fancy placed the back of her hand over her mouth, shielding the raucous laughter that pushed forward. "I'm not laughing, but then again, yes I am. She actually stood up, in the pulpit, at the mic, and started preaching? Lord, I've heard it all. I'm sorry, Stiles, this is way too much for me to digest. I need a good stiff Pepsi after hearing that."

Stiles chuckled but then he bore a straight face. Glaring at Fancy, he rose from the sofa. "It's not funny when I think about it," Stiles said before disappearing into the kitchen.

Minutes later he returned to the family room with a tall glass of Pepsi on ice.

"Here you go, my lady." He flashed a dazzling smile as he gave her the glass and paper napkin.

"You surprised me with this. I didn't see you bring a soda with you when you came in." She giggled, readily accepting the glass.

"I can't let you know all my secrets."

"Yeah, I know," she smiled. Does Hezekiah know what she did?" Her expression turned serious.

"You know it. He's keeping a level head, at least from what I can tell. He has Trevor Price, you know the same lawyer who was Xavier's attorney, and he's going to handle the divorce."

Fancy exhaled, and took a swallow of Pepsi. "Ahhh, this is *sooo* good," then she took another swallow. "I'm glad he's divorcing her crazy self."

"He's also doing the paperwork to be Hezekiah's Power of Attorney."

"His what?"

"You know, Power of Attorney," Stiles repeated.

"Uh, is that a good thing? Doesn't making someone your power of attorney give them the right to act on your behalf, or actually it means they in essence take *your* place. I don't know if that's a smart move or not," Fancy queried.

"Look, Price is a good lawyer. I don't think Hezekiah could have chosen a better guy, especially since he needs someone trustworthy to look out for his best interests. He had to find a way to stop Rianna. The woman is spending his money like rushing water pouring from a waterfall. She's charged thousands of dollars on his cards. Uses his money to pay for that apartment she still has over there near Mud

Island, not to mention all her other bills. She's atrocious."

"This is hard to hear. I know he's done a lot he has to pay for. I don't know if you call it vengeance, retribution or whatever, and even though he and I have had our bad times, I still don't wish any ill will on him," she paused and then continued. "He's worked hard to get what he has. He built up Holy Rock and before he was sent away he was building up New Holy Rock. I was starting to see a change in him. You know, for the better."

"Yeah, it's hard to watch everything unfolding like this, but I keep praying and I'm believing God's going to work it all out. He's the one that has the final say, but that's not all. Maybe this will make you feel better."

"What?"

"They found the person responsible for shooting him."

"My God, who? Who did it? Is it anyone we know, that I know?"

"I don't know if you know him. His name is Vernon...Vernon Clay. They used to be members of Holy Rock a long time ago. He's your stepson's stepdad."

"Are you talking about Hezekiah's outside child?"

"Yes, I didn't know how much you knew about that."

"Not much; I just know he had a kid while we were married. Nothing he does ceases to amaze me, but is that the Vernon you're talking about?"

"Yes, that's him. The boy's mother's name is Mariah."

"I saw a picture of her, but I can't say I remember her from Holy Rock."

"Okay, well, he confessed. Said Hezekiah ruined his family. He said Hezekiah went around telling everybody that he was a pedophile."

"What?" Fancy slapped a hand to her forehead and jumped up from the sofa, quickly placing the half glass of Pepsi on a nearby table. "This...this is all too much. Am I living in a Lifetime movie or what? Is it true? Is the man a sex offender for real?"

Stiles got up and walked up behind her, placing a hand on each side of her shoulders. "I know this is a lot for you to take in. But yes, it's true; he served time for it some years ago. Hezekiah wasn't lying, I'm so sorry, Fancy."

She turned and faced Stiles with a half-smile. "It's not your fault. I'm just overwhelmed." She started sobbing into her hands.

Stiles wrapped himself around her and soothed her until he felt her body relax against his. He held her until she was ready to ease out of his arms.

When she was done crying, she picked up her glass of Pepsi, and returned to the sofa. She turned up the glass, took several swallows until the glass was empty, and focused on Stiles with red puffy eyes. "You know what they say..."

"No, tell me, what do *they* say," Stiles replied somberly.

"We may not always understand God's timing, but we have to trust that his timing is perfect."

nineteen

"A deceitful tongue will always be good at twisting the truth." Dennis Adonis

Rianna dropped Tiny off at home, stopped at Olive Garden, and placed a takeout order. When she presented her credit card for payment, once again, it was declined. She had to use her debit card again.

Did Hezekiah have something to do with any of this? As if that wasn't enough, she drove around the corner and went inside the Bundt Cake store. This time when her card was declined rather than using her debit card to pay, she intimidated the cashier by going into a tirade.

"Enough is enough, darn it! Just keep it. I don't want it! This itty-bitty darn cake cost too much anyway. This ain't no bigger than a cupcake," she screamed at the frightened Asian woman behind the counter. She hissed and turned around, almost knocking over an older gray-haired woman standing behind her as she stormed out the store.

When she arrived at Lion's Gate, she bolted inside, barely closing the garage door leading into the house, threw her purse to the side, and sat on a bar stool at the kitchen island. Pulling out each of her credit cards, she called customer service. Each time she grew more furious after being told no information could be given other than usage on the cards was restricted.

After the last call she made and hearing the same response, Rianna shook her head, rolled her eyes, inhaled and slammed the phone face down on the granite counter top, cracking the phone screen. "Ahhhhh!"

She took off through the house like hurricane force winds. Clothing went in every direction all over her bedroom as she flung a blouse here, a dress there, pants over in another corner, undergarments on the bed. With one hand and a swoop all her toiletries and accessories on her dresser crashed to the hardwood floor, while some landed on the Oriental rug. She screamed and cussed as she went about destroying the room and emptying all of her drawers.

"You're going to pay for what you've done, Hezekiah McCoy. Oh, yes, baby, you're going to pay dearly, you bastard!"

†

Rianna drove like a bat out of hell in the direction of New Holy Rock. It was early evening. Stiles should still be at the church office.

When she arrived, she was relieved when she saw his car in front of the entrance. She parked, jumped out of her car, and raced to the front door. Inserting her key, she started banging on the door and pressing the buzzer when her key failed to unlock the doors of New Holy Rock.

After abusing the buzzer again and again finally one of the building engineers came to the door and opened it.

"Why won't my key work?" Rianna barked at the young man who looked no more than nineteen or twenty years old.

"I'm sorry, First Lady, I was told to change all the locks. I did what Pastor Graham told me to do," he said apologetically.

"Well, you better make a set for me. I'm the First Lady and don't you ever forget it," she said, not toning down her aggressiveness as she inched toward the obviously scared young man.

"Yes…yes, ma'am," he said and scurried off.

Rianna trailed up the church hallway and did not stop until she was standing in front of the door with the sign: PASTOR STILES GRAHAM – ASSOCIATE PASTOR

Without knocking, she turned the knob—the door opened. She pounced inside, taking Stiles by surprise.

Stiles swirled around in his chair, the office phone still plastered to his ear. His eyes widened when he saw Rianna standing before him looking like an angry mother lion.

"Uh, Pastor Gibbs, if you don't mind, can I call you back," Stiles said and ended the call.

"What can I do for you, Sista Rianna?" he asked calmly while clasping his hands and resting his elbows on top of his desk.

"You and your brother have some nerves, Stiles. You won't get away with what you're doing," Rianna said, shouting.

"First, I suggest you calm down. Take a seat."

Rianna grunted, but she yanked the chair and plopped down in it.

After she took her seat, Stiles continued. "Now, I'll answer any questions you have."

"You had the nerve to change the locks on this church. Are you a fool? Do you know I operate on my husband's behalf? I'm the one who runs this church. Not you, Stiles." She poked her own chest. "I told that boy you call a building engineer to get me a set of keys made pronto."

"That won't be happening, Rianna. The board met and it has been voted on and decided by the majority that you are no longer on the staff of New Holy Rock. You are of course still the First Lady, legally, but my brother is working on dissolving that as we speak," Stiles said, maintaining a straight face and a calm tone which seemed to make Rianna that much madder.

She twisted and turned in the seat before Stiles. "You think y'all can get away with this? Well you won't! No way. And my credit cards? How do you expect me to live? What am I supposed to do about money?"

"I guess you should have figured that out while you were collecting Hezekiah's salary and other benefits. All I can say is welcome to the big leagues, First Lady. Sometimes the ball doesn't always roll in your favor."

"How dare you talk to me like that you sorry, good for nothing, wanna be your brother so bad, miserable, unhappy fool. You'll never amount to nothing. You'll never be Hezekiah McCoy, not ever. You'll always be in his shadow!" Rianna continued to swear.

Stiles listened and watched, trying to maintain his cool, while underneath he was growing angrier and angrier. He hoped Rianna would just shut up and leave. His prayer was soon answered.

Rianna sprung out of the chair, kicked it over, and then ran toward the door. Stopping at the door, she turned and gave Stiles the most evil look then swore, "You better tell your brother he messed with the wrong chick. I'm not like that weak tail, Fancy. I won't roll over and whimper. No, buddy, not me. Not Rianna Jamison....McCoy. But I can show y'all betta than I can tell ya." With that, she opened the door and it popped back against the office wall. Rianna disappeared like a thief in the night.

†

The following morning, Rianna got up and climbed over the pile of clothing and other items still strewn across the room. She dragged herself to the bathroom where there was even more stuff lining the tile floors.

She managed to reach the shower, and found some relaxation under the hot jet streams pouring down on her from the rain shower.

After sorting through the mess of clothes, she found a pair of leggings, sneakers, a colorful top and light jacket. Next, she went to the kitchen and made herself a strong cup of black coffee, something she hardly ever drank. But she needed something strong to wake her up. She had a full day and a long drive ahead of her.

When she left the house the sun was beginning to showcase its beauty over the Mississippi River. The stars had all but disappeared and a blue sky was pushing through as the rays splendidly rose up over the horizon. It was destined to be a beautiful fall day.

She opened her sunroof, allowing the crisp air to bathe her smooth melanin skin and blow her long weave in the air from side to side. Along the way, she stopped at the phone store to buy a replacement phone. Once again, her card was declined. The clerk agreed to add the cost of the phone to Rianna's phone plan.

Leaving the phone store, she got back inside her car and took off toward the hills of Pikeville and Spencer where the correctional center was nestled between.

Tapping the button on the steering wheel a few times, she stopped channel scanning when she heard a CeCe Winans song. She turned up the volume, raising her hands in praise while singing every word of the song like she was CeCe reincarnated.

A little under five hours after leaving Memphis, she was in front of the entrance to Bledsoe County Correctional Facility. She glanced at her dashboard clock. 10:17 A.M. Hezekiah could start receiving visitors in less than an hour and she was going to be first, front and center. She came armed with an arsenal of questions she wanted answers to. At the top of that list was where the heck was her money.

Just as she predicted, she was one of the first people in line. She watched to her left and to her right as cars started flooding into the visitors' parking lot. She shook her head and smiled.

"The early bird catches the...uh...the uh something," she mumbled and stopped when the CO told her to place her personal items on the moving tray. She did.

When she passed through screening, she was stopped by another CO who looked for her name on the visitor's log. As she stood there, Rianna noticed it was taking longer than usual. Every other time, it took less than a couple of minutes. She shrugged her shoulders and then looked in front of her. That's when she noticed the CO had gone into the office next to where visitor's sign in. She saw him talking to a busty female corrections officer sitting behind a raggedy wooden desk.

Rianna continued spying through the office window despite it having smudges of nasty fingerprint smears and other particles on it.

The CO finally reappeared. "Ma'am, step over here."

Rianna, rolling her eyes, did as she was told.

"Uh, ma'am, you are not on the visitor's list. You have to leave," he said barely looking at Rianna while pushing her ID back toward her.

"Nah, there's gotta be a mistake. Plus, you know me. I've been coming to this prison for almost two freaking years. What do you mean I'm not on the visitor's list? Did you look under Hezekiah McCoy? Inmate number..." and she rattled off his inmate number.

"Ma'am, your name has been removed at the inmate's request." This time the CO rolled his eyes and gave her a nasty look. "You have to leave—now." The officer was stern and pointed toward the sign that read EXIT.

Rianna whirled around. Other visitors in line stared at her, some mumbled, and others giggled under their breath, making fun of her dilemma.

She took off almost in a gallop outside the building, onto the parking lot, and to her car. Inside the car, she hit the steering wheel, pounding it repeatedly with both hands. One cuss word after another flowed effortlessly from her mouth as she zoomed out of the parking lot.

After driving for about an hour, she turned off the exit with gas and food signs. She topped off her car with gas and then went inside to the small diner connected to the gas station. She ordered a soda, a breakfast sandwich, some tater tots, and sat at one of the empty tables. Picking over her food, she called Tiny, knowing she was probably already at work.

"Hello," Tiny answered. "You still on the road?"

"Yeah, I'm on the road alright, on the road back to Memphis."

"Huh? Back to Memphis? Already?"

"Girl, can you believe that dog-faced punk took me off his visitor's list. I made a five hour trip up to this godforsaken place for nothing, Tiny. I'm so freaking mad," she hollered into the phone.

"Settle down, are you sure they didn't make some kinda mistake? Those CO's don't give a dang about nobody's feelings. They be looking over that list so fast. They probably passed over your name."

"That's what I was thinking at first, but nah, Hezekiah took me off. The officer checked with the main office. Hezekiah had requested my name be removed and I was not to be given any more information about him. Then they told me I had to leave."

"Dang, girl. That's messed up. Whatchu gon' do now?"

"I don't know. I'll think of something. You at work?"

"Yeah, and I'm starting to get a line so I gotta go. I'll try to call you on my break."

"Okay, bye, girl."

She drove for another fifteen or twenty minutes and then decided to call Big Daddy. "Please answer," she pleaded aloud. "Please, please, please," she said as raindrops started dancing on her car.

"What do you want?"

"Oh, Abel, I'm so glad you answered," she cried.

"Look, I told you not to call me," he grumbled.

"Will you just listen for a minute," she pleaded. She told him all about her money being cut off and her credit card access being denied. She let him know that Hezekiah was trying to divorce her and cut her off from everything. "I'm going to need your help, Big Daddy. Just for a while, just until I can get things worked out with Hezekiah. You know me, I'm not about to let him screw me around. No, not me."

"I can't help you anymore," Abel said, peeping quickly over his shoulder and whispering. "Look, you're on your own. Now don't make me block you, Rianna. Don't call me again."

The facetime screen went blue. Rianna for a second stared at the screen before bursting in tears.

As she drove, the skies quickly went from the sun shining to dark storm clouds looming. It didn't take but a few minutes after Rianna was headed home when fierce winds started and a flurry of thunderstorms filtered across the sky. Fist sized splashes of rain attacked her car and soon thereafter baseball size hail was hitting it so hard that Rianna thought it was going to come through her roof or bust out her car windows.

Lately, a vast portion of Tennessee had been experiencing unusual weather. Almost every day it was either cold as cold could get or rainy, dark, and dreary. Today, it was a *raining cats and dogs* kind of day. Thunder rumbled across the southern skies and the ferocious wind shook Rianna's luxury vehicle causing it to sway as she fought to maintain control.

She drove along the blinding road, tears pouring hard as the rain down her cheeks. Through her tears and the foggy windshield, she tried to follow the white shiny round things lining the street. A couple of times, because the rain was so heavy, and the winds so strong, she swerved almost crossing the median. Car horns blew as they passed.

"Shut up!" she swore. "Ugh, why did I even come this way?" she screamed as she checked to make sure her wipers were set on HIGH, but they proved not to be strong enough to push back the heavy rain.

She tried seeing through the side mirrors but they were fogged up too. Finally, she was able to catch a glimpse of her blind spot. When she didn't see a car or anything coming, she made the switch to get in the right lane so she could take the next exit, but her sight was heavily impaired. Bright beams of light appeared but she couldn't tell if they were from in front of her or behind her. *Oh, God, what's that deafening noise? Did someone have an accident? Oh, God what happened?* Rianna was met with darkness.

twenty

"Deceit's favorite role is playing the victim."
Unknown

The day arrived for the first official gathering of *The Pulpit Ladies Ministry*. Today was the beginning of what Eliana believed was a ministry ordained by God, a culmination of all the efforts she had made to bring the ministry into fruition.

Twenty-five first ladies from churches throughout the city were expected to attend the invitation only luncheon in the banquet hall at Holy Rock. She envisioned it growing into a national organization and ministry that welcomed women of faith regardless of denomination. Today—25. Tomorrow—2,500.

"Everything looks absolutely perfect," Eliana beamed while walking around each table and complimenting the decorations and layout.

"I think we did a pretty good job," Pepper said, standing next to Eliana.

"Me too," another one of the ladies agreed.

"We're expecting twenty-five ladies today, but I believe God is going to bless this ministry so quick and fast that before we know it we'll be hosting thousands," Eliana said, beaming.

"Amen, speak it into existence, First Lady," another one of the women added.

At the end of the two-hour luncheon, Eliana and her crew felt accomplished that today's event was a walloping success. There were some things Eliana felt could be improved upon, like the menu to include more options, more diverse topic selection, and some other suggestions that were discussed during the luncheon. It was a chance for her to hear suggestions and opinions of the women in attendance. She was sure to take their suggestions into full consideration to make *The Pulpit Ladies* a one of its kind ministry.

Her fears or concerns about Detria Graham showing her face at today's luncheon had been unknowingly thwarted by none other than Sista Mavis.

Sista Mavis promised Eliana that she was going to be a gatekeeper and make sure ladies like Detria Graham didn't come barging in crashing the luncheon.

True to the game, Detria made an attempt. It wouldn't be like her if she didn't. She had given special consideration to what she was going to wear. She proudly strolled into Holy Rock, caught the elevator to the downstairs banquet hall, but before she could barely step off the elevator she was greeted by none other than Sista Mavis.

"And where do you think you're going?" Sista Mavis with hands on her hips posted herself in front of Detria when she stepped off the elevator and into the hallway.

"Last time I checked, I don't recall you being in charge of anything...or anybody," Detria spouted.

"Look, I try to be a good Christian woman, but women like you make it hard," Sista Mavis growled. "Now you know and I know that you don't belong here. You ain't been nobody's first lady in years, and even then you weren't worthy to wear the title, but I ain't one to judge. I just call 'em like I see 'em. And you," Sista Mavis continued with her verbal beat down, "ain't here to do nothing but make trouble and cause a scene. Now you turn yourself around and get on out of here," Sista Mavis demanded.

Detria put up the act like she was standing her ground, but the tremble in her voice and her eyes bulging told the real story.

"Look here old lady, lucky for you I don't feel like fooling with you today." Detria rolled her eyes, pressed the elevator button, and pronto the doors opened and she scooted back inside.

"You have a good day," Sista Mavis smarted off. With arms folded and her lips poked out, she retained her stance, waiting until the elevator doors closed.

†

Detria was furious. Sitting in the front driveway of her home, she facetimed her sister and told her about her encounter with Sista Mavis.

"Brooke, I'm telling you that old biddy better be glad she was up in the church 'cause if she was anywhere else I would have drug her big behind from one end of the hallway to the other. Just who the heck does she think she is putting me out the church? That church wouldn't be able to do half the stuff it does if it wasn't for the money I pour into that den of thieves."

"Well, if you feel like that you're the fool. No way I would be paying my money to a church that doesn't respect me, let alone one where members like Sista Mavis thinks she runs the place. I don't know why you still go there. Of all the thousands of churches in this city and you have to stay at that one, all because of some no good man you're messing off with," Brooke chastised her.

"After the way I was just treated, I might just do that. I might move my membership someplace where I'm appreciated. And Khalil doesn't want to have anything to do with me but yet he wants to call himself a man of God. Girl, please. Ever since that wife of his had that brat he wanna play *daddy day care* or something. Well, if he don't want me then I sure as heck don't want him."

Looking at her sister on the screen, Brooke sighed, shook her head, and pursed her lips. "I hope you mean that because you can do better. Preacher or no preacher, that man is no good for you, Dee. He ought to be ashamed of himself, standing up in a pulpit Sunday after Sunday telling folks about God, but sleeping with his church members. It's shameful. I keep telling you that you need to stop messing with other folk's men and husbands. You and I both know it's not right, Dee."

"I can't help that these men who come after me end up having women or wives or whatever."

"Yeah, but you don't have to talk to them," Brooke shot back. "You're getting too old for all this unnecessary drama in your life. Speaking of drama, have you talked to Momma?"

"Yeah, day before yesterday. Why, what's going on with her? She's okay isn't she? Is it her high blood pressure? Half the time she doesn't eat right so I wouldn't be surprised if it's high."

"Nah, she's doing okay health wise. Of course, you know she still eats what she wants when she wants, but I was talking about if she told you that Skip came by her house yesterday. He brought Elijah to see her."

"Okay, *and?* What's unusual about that?"

"It's nothing unusual for him to bring him to see his grandmother, but he told Momma they're moving at the end of the month. He's opening two new Subway franchises; one in Nashville and one in Gatlinburg. They're going to move somewhere up there. He's still going to keep the two Subways he has here. He told Momma that his business partner is going to manage them."

Detria shrugged. "I don't keep up with him or else I get mad all over again when I think about how I gave him the money and set him up to get his first Subway. Now look at him. He thinks he and that ugly tale wife of his are Kim and Kanye."

"Sis, you are so crazy." Brooke burst into laughter. "But what do you think about him moving?"

"I don't care one way or the other."

"Not even about Elijah. He's your son, Detria. You need to—"

"Stop right there, Brooke. I don't wanna hear what I *need* to do. Just 'cause I gave birth to him don't make him my son. He's Skip's kid.

I keep telling you that. Unlike you, I am not mommy material. I don't wanna hear nothing else about it. But while we're talking about Skip and Elijah, I've been meaning to tell y'all something for a minute. I guess I thought by now Skip woulda told y'all."

"Told us what? What have you gone and done now, Dee?"

"Nothing bad, so don't worry. A while back, well more than a while back, Skip asked me about signing away my parental rights so that Meaghan could legally adopt Elijah."

"What? Is he crazy? Please tell me you aren't considering doing that, Dee?"

"No, I'm not considering it."

Brooke exhaled with relief. "Good."

"I already did it."

"You what? You did it? You signed your rights away? Are you crazy?"

"Why wouldn't I? The boy doesn't care two cents about me. He already calls Meaghan his mother and I rarely if ever see him. *Shooot*, y'all see him more than I do, which is cool by me. I can't help if raising kids is not on my bucket list. I don't have the patience, energy or the desire to play *mommy dearest*. And before you say anything, yes I got pregnant, but that was not intentional. Do you honestly think I want to be responsible for a kid after what happened to my little girl? She's dead, Brooke, and there's nothing I can do about that. Nah, let them give Elijah the life I don't choose to give him. I paid him child support every month without fail. Now that he has all the rights I don't even have to do that. You, Momma and Daddy can talk about me and be mad all you want but I did what was best for my kid."

"Nah, you did what was best for Detria, like you always do. I can't listen to any more of this foolish talk. Not now. I can't believe you would do something like that. Poor Elijah."

"Poor Elijah nothing. What part of *my son doesn't like me* don't you understand? He's doing just fine with his daddy and stepmama."

"Suit yourself, crazy girl. Look, I've got to go. I need to finish cooking. John and the boys will be coming home shortly."

"Okay, bye Brooke. Love you."

"Love you too," Brooke sadly replied.

twenty-one

"Don't be bothered by troubles. They are generally guests we ourselves invite."
Amit Abraham

Tiny called Rianna again. No response. She had not answered phone, facetime calls, or texts.

"What's going on with you, Rianna?" Tiny spoke aloud as she called her friend. Initially, the phone would ring several times before going to voicemail but now it was going immediately to her voicemail. Tiny took that as an indication that either Rianna had turned off her phone or it had gone dead.

She grew increasingly worried. There was no one she knew to call who would tell her anything. Rianna had no friends other than the acquaintances she'd met at New Holy Rock, but Tiny didn't know any of those folks.

"Rianna, where are you?" she asked, concern rising in her voice. "I hope you haven't gone and gotten yourself in any kinda trouble." The last time they spoke, Rianna said she was headed home from making a blank trip to see Hezekiah. After she learned upon arriving that he'd removed her from the visitor's list, she left infuriated and Tiny hadn't heard from her since.

"I hope you didn't go and do nothing crazy and got yourself locked up," Tiny continued talking aloud as she drove to pick up her son from school.

Later that evening, at the end of the day, Tiny called Rianna again. Nothing.

She said a short awkward prayer asking God to take care of her friend. "Amen," she said, ending her prayer and pulling the bedcovers up around her neck.

†

Rianna forced her eyes to open. It was as if concrete blocks were resting on top of her eyelids. Slowly, each one cracked open. It hurt just to open them, but she willed herself to look around the unfamiliar space. Where in the heck was she? What happened? Had she been kidnapped? She tried moving but every inch of movement caused her to wince in pain. She managed to raise her head a hair inch and suddenly came to the realization she was lifting her head off of a pillow.

Had she overslept? Was she dreaming or what? The last thing she recalled was being told she had to leave Bledsoe Correctional Facility because Hezekiah's low down behind had taken her off his visitor's list. She remembered driving along highway 127 headed toward Highway 72 which would lead her right back home to Memphis.

Puzzled, she continued to try and remember her last steps from the time she left Bledsoe to her waking up in this strange place. The clock to the right of her hanging on the white wall said the time was 1:47. "One forty-seven," she said mumbling through her pasty lips and mouth. *But that would mean I've only been gone from Bledsoe a little over an hour? That's it? What am I doing here then? God, what's going on? This doesn't make sense.* Her brain kept feeding her conflicting stories.

She glanced a little over her head to her left and saw a machine and IV line. Was she in a hospital? If so, why? She eased her head up a little more and saw the white sheets covering her and one leg propped up on one of those thingamajigs hospitals used for patients with broken legs or arms, whatever.

Hanging on the side of the railed hospital bed, she noticed a long white cord resembling a phone charger. She recognized it as the cord to call the nurse or change television channels. After a struggle she was able to reach it and press the CALL button.

"You're awake," the nurse said when she entered Rianna's room and stood at the side of her bed.

Rianna struggled with her speech, and her head pounded like a fresh set of boulders had been dropped on top of it. She could hardly move and the pain was excruciating. Screaming out, she asked the nurse for help.

"Shhh, hun, I'll get you something for the pain," the blue-haired nurse with a soothing angelic like voice assured Rianna.

"Where...where am I? What happened?"

"You were in a pretty bad accident. You're at Erlanger Bledsoe Hospital. You're one lucky gal. God was definitely with you. The car you were in from what I was told was burned to a crisp."

Rianna blindly looked at the nurse, not fully comprehending what the nurse was talking about. *Accident? Burned? Lucky to be alive?* All the things the nurse said, twirled around in Rianna's head, swirling about like bees surrounding a beehive.

"Let me go get you something for the pain. I'll be right back."

True to her word, moments later, she returned and began putting something into Rianna's IV.

Rianna drifted back into the world of unconsciousness.

†

This time when Rianna woke up, the clock read 6:22. The room was almost dark except for the picture window that displayed trees and scattered buildings across the horizon as far as the little bit Rianna could see.

Like before, she was prepared to press the CALL button, but at that time the door opened and in walked two white coated men. One was a typical looking white guy and the second one, a rather striking man with shoulder length black hair and thick eyebrows who was nothing short of a European hunk.

“Hello, there, lucky lady,” the hunk said as both doctors approached taking stances on opposite sides of her hospital bed.

“Do you remember what happened?” the plain looking doctor asked.

Rianna shook her head and whispered, “No.”

“Well, you were in a serious one car crash off highway 127. Your car jumped the guardrail and ended up in a ravine where it exploded. We don’t know how you made it out but you did.”

“Can you tell us your name? Any identification, purse, phone, everything was lost in the fire, we assume.”

Rianna’s eyes shifted from one doctor to the other. “Rianna....Rianna Ja...McCoy,” she mumbled.

"Rianna Jacoy? Did I hear that correctly?" the hunk asked.

"McCoy," she repeated.

"Well then, Ms. McCoy, we're going to keep you as comfortable as possible. You've already been to surgery. You have a number of fractures, including a fractured right femur, left fractured meniscus, left and right ankle fractures, and a fractured left wrist."

"You have several surgeries ahead of you," the hunk added. "and a lengthy recovery but the good news is you should make a full recovery." He half smiled.

"I do want to caution you that you sustained some facial injuries," the plain looking doctor explained.

"What...what kind of facial injuries?" Rianna tried to raise a hand to her face but was unable to do so. Tears formed and were quickly absorbed into her dehydrated face.

"Shh, don't worry about that now," he spoke softly.

"Just so you know we won't be keeping you here. This is only a 25-bed nursing unit plus the trauma room, where you are now. You'll be transported to Vanderbilt Hospital in Nashville which is a little over two hours away. A transport will pick you up later this morning. You'll be in good hands. Don't worry." The hunk smiled.

"Oh, okay. Did...you say mor...ning? I thought...What day is this? How long have I..."

"It's Friday morning. You've been here three days, Ms. McCoy, but don't worry, you're in good hands. Is there someone the nurse can call for you? Husband? Family? Anyone?"

Rianna slowly nodded.

"Okay, good, we'll send the nurse in to collect that information and contact your family right away. In the meantime, we want you to get some rest. The transport service should be here soon." The hunk lightly patted her right hand and the two doctors exited the room.

Twenty something minutes later, a social worker arrived. Rianna gave the social worker as much information as she could remember about herself, Hezekiah, and who the social worker could notify. She didn't recall anyone's phone numbers. Not Tiny and not Abel, not that Abel would come.

"Call...brother-in-law at New Holy Rock in Memphis," she muttered.

"Okay, good, I'll do that right away." The social worker looked up from her tablet as the hospital door opened and she met eyes with two men and one female who entered. Their uniforms revealed they were from the transport service.

"Don't you worry; I'll get in touch with your brother-in-law. I'll let the social worker at the prison know too. She'll be the one to inform your husband. Shortly after you arrive at Vanderbilt, a worker from the Patient Advocacy Department will come see you. I'll make sure they have the information you gave me."

Rianna half-smiled as *concrete boulders* rested again on her eyelids, forcing them to close. A nurse had come in while the social worker was talking and injected pain medication into her IV in preparation for the ride ahead. Minutes later she was in *la la* land.

twenty-two

"Selfishness and greed cause most of our troubles." Harry Truman

Hezekiah was summoned to the social worker's cage-like office where he was given the news about Rianna. Unknown by him at the time, the same afternoon Stiles had been contacted by a social worker from Vanderbilt Hospital who told him about Rianna's accident. Stiles went into prayer for her as soon as the man informed him of the seriousness of her injuries.

"Thank God she's alive," Stiles said, standing and pacing the floor of his church office. He had been uploading lessons for his online class when the call came in. "I'll be up there as soon as I can. In the meantime, if you can keep me updated or give me some information so I can call and check on her in the hospital. Is there a phone in her room?"

"Yes sir, there's a phone in her room, but she's physically unable to answer at this time. She can barely talk. Plus, she's in a lot of pain so they keep her sedated. She's scheduled to have multiple surgeries over the next two weeks. But I will pass your information on to the attending physician and the nurse's station. They'll be able to tell you more about visitation and of course about her condition."

"Thank you. Thank you very much. God Bless you." Stiles ended the call, nervously rubbed his head back and forth as he went and sat on the edge of his desk.

The social worker also told him that Hezekiah had been informed earlier that day about Rianna. Stiles hoped he would hear from his brother soon. He needed to see what frame of mind Hezekiah was in after hearing the news.

He gathered some items, contacted his administrative assistant, and then left the church heading home. When he made it home, he called Fancy and gave her the news.

"I'm sorry to hear about that," Fancy said. "I'll be sure to pray for her. I wonder if Hezekiah knows."

"Yes, the social worker said he did."

"I wonder how he's dealing with that. Where are you?" Fancy inquired.

"At home. For now. I'm going to drive to Nashville in the morning. Someone needs to check on Rianna. She may not be the best liked person, but she's my brother's wife. He can't be there so that leaves me."

"What about that girl she's always with. I think her name is something like Teeny, Peeny, Tiny, I don't know. But isn't she a member of New Holy Rock? Maybe you can find her contact information on the church roster."

"Nah, she's never joined. Not that I know of. I know she visits often. That's about it. But I can still get my assistant or Xavier to search the church database. Maybe she paid money and gave her name. Either way, that's a good suggestion. I'll get on it."

"Do you want me to ride up there with you? I don't mind, really I don't. I have nothing special planned for tomorrow or this weekend," Fancy offered.

"I don't think so. I don't want to drag you into this. I know uh, Rianna is not one of your favorite people."

"No, she isn't. That doesn't even describe it. But like you said, she needs someone there for her. After all, it's our Christian duty to love the unlovable," she said, chuckling. "Seriously, I know I would hate to be laid up in a hospital facing surgery and no one's there for me or concerned about me. I don't wish that on any human being, no matter how evil or mean that person is. And hey, I don't have to physically go *see* her. I'm riding up there to keep *you* company, not to go see Rianna. I don't want to get her upset like that. 'Cause just like she's not my favorite person, I'm not exactly at the top of her favorite people list either."

It was Stiles' turn to laugh and he chuckled into the phone. "Yeah, you have a point."

"She doesn't have to know I'm in Nashville. I can go shopping. I've been wanting to drive back up to Green Hills Mall for months, and just have not done it."

"Oh, so the truth is revealed. You're going to use me to hitch a free ride, huh?" He continued laughing.

"Uh, dang, you caught me," Fancy said. "Really, I'll be glad to ride with you." Fancy giggled. "What do you say? You want company?"

Stiles listened, paused, and then spoke. "Can you be ready at around seven in the morning?"

"I will be awaiting my chariot," she joked before ending the call.

†

"I'm glad you came," Stiles said as they traveled Interstate 40 toward Nashville.

"Anytime you want a ride along, give me a call. I don't mind, Stiles." Fancy reached over and affectionately patted his forearm.

"I'll remember that. As I was saying earlier, Hezekiah called right as I was walking out the door to pick you up."

"How did he sound? Does he know about Rianna?"

"Yeah, he said they let him know. Of course, he was concerned, but he was straight. I told him I was driving up to see her. He was glad to hear that. I can't go see him because it's not visitation day, so that's out of the question. That would have been another two plus hours on the other side anyway."

"I'm just glad he's good, and I'm glad you didn't tell him I was riding with you."

"Oh, but I did. He knows it had to take a lot for you to offer to ride up here with me. He said as much. He just didn't want nothing popping off at the hospital between you and Rianna. I told him you weren't actually going to go to the hospital with me. He sounded relieved to hear that." Stiles paused and then smiled. "My brother still loves you, Fancy." Stiles glanced over at Fancy and she met him with a knowing glance of her own.

"I wouldn't say all that." She looked out her window.

"You already did." He focused back on the road.

"Any word about the POA?" she asked, changing the tense subject.

"Only that everything is moving forward as it should. The divorce has been filed. Although I don't know how or if this accident will affect the outcome of the proceedings."

"He's probably going to have to pay alimony and we know her hospital bills, depending on insurance, but from the financial part it depends on how much he's worth. Probably not much left since he married her," Fancy huffed, shook her head and stared blankly out the window.

"Don't get upset. At the end of the day, what I've learned about my brother is he always, and I mean always has a ram somewhere hidden in a bush."

Fancy smiled and looked at Stiles. "So true."

They kept the conversation lively, listened to some pop gospel songs, and said a prayer for Rianna, Hezekiah, and their loved ones. Before they both knew it, Stiles ventured to the right toward the VANDERBILT HOSPITAL EXIT.

"Call me when you want me to head back this way."

"You sure you're going to be good?" Stiles pulled and stopped in the circular DROP OFF area.

"Oh yeah, your riding partner is about to go get her shop on."

"Cool, see you in a couple of hours—I mean I'll call. Have fun."

Fancy waited while Stiles sprinted to her side of the car and opened the door. "Thanks. See you later."

She stood and watched as he went through the double automatic hospital doors before she walked around and got into the car. Another car pulled up just as she closed the door. The person blew their horn.

Shaking her head and looking briefly in her side mirror, she put the car in DRIVE and with a big smile plastered across her dimpled face drove in the direction of The Mall at Green Hills.

On her way to the mall, Victoria called Fancy.

"Where are you? I'm at your house, ringing the doorbell."

"*Whaaat*? Did I miss something Were we supposed to be doing something today?"

"Girl, nah, I'm just messing with you. I'm still at work."

Fancy exhaled. "I'm in Nashville."

"Nashville? Okay, now who's fooling who?"

"I'm not fooling. I was intending to call you, but it honestly slipped my mind."

"What's going on? Why are you in Nashville?"

"Rianna was in a bad car accident. She's in Vanderbilt Hospital. Stiles said she was on her way back to Memphis after visiting Hezekiah. He got the call from the hospital. She's in serious condition. From what we understand, she has to have several surgeries. That's about all I know. I rode up here with him to keep him company. Just dropped him off at the hospital and I'm on my way to Green Hills. Gonna do a little window shopping."

Victoria laughed into the phone. "Girl, please. You and I both know you're going to do some damage at those high end stores up there. And I'll say a prayer for Rianna. She may be a witch but I don't wish anything bad for her."

"Right, neither do I. Well, I'll call you later. I'll probably wait until after we get back to Memphis, which probably won't be until later this evening or tonight."

"Okay, I'm going to the gym after I get off, so we'll talk tonight or tomorrow. Tell Stiles I said hello."

"Okay, will do. Talk to you later."

†

Stiles immediately began praying in his spirit when he witnessed the fragile, swollen, and unconscious Rianna. She looked like a ghost. Facial bandages on one side of her red grossly swollen face, made her unrecognizable. Casts and tractions were on one arm while pins and rods protruded from both of her ankles.

He cautiously approached her bed. The ICU nurse told him he would need to keep his visit short. No more than a few minutes. He had miscalculated his visitation time way too much when he told Fancy to give him at least two hours. He didn't give account that she would be in the ICU Trauma Unit and unconscious. Standing at her bedside, he watched her as she slept.

"I'm ready. short visit I know, sis," he texted Fancy.

Moments later his text notifier dinged. "OTW giv me thirty min."

Stiles answered Fancy's text with a thumbs-up emoji and then tucked away his phone in his inside jacket pocket.

"Rianna," he whispered, "it's Stiles. Stiles Graham."

Rianna stirred. Several seconds passed.

"You don't have to open your eyes. You don't have to say a word. Just know that someone is here for you. I'm here. I'm praying for you and New Holy Rock is praying for you."

Rianna stirred again. This time her eyelids fluttered and then slowly opened—halfway. More fluttering.

Stiles smiled and gently rested his hand on her arm. “Hello, First Lady.”

He watched as she tried to open her mouth. Nothing came out other than a slight grunt.

“Shhh, don’t try to speak. Get your rest. You just came out of surgery a few hours ago. Would you like it if I said a prayer with you?”

She barely nodded.

Stiles said a short but effective prayer. Tears crested in her eyes. He tenderly squeezed her mid-arm and kissed her forehead.

Rianna drifted back off to sleep.

A nurse appeared behind him, rested her hand on his shoulder, and whispered, “She needs to get her rest. You can visit again in a few hours.”

“Ok,” he whispered and then turned back toward Rianna. “God bless you, Rianna.” Stiles turned, half-smiled, and walked out of the room. He stopped at the nurse’s station to make sure they had his contact information before he boarded the elevator.

twenty-three

"It's not the tragedies that kill us, it's the messes." D. Parker

Thirteen days after the accident, Rianna was transferred to the hospital's rehab facility to undergo intense rehabilitative, occupational, and speech therapy. There she would remain 15 to 30 days.

Stiles remained in contact with the hospital and now he would do the same with the rehab facility. His last visit was the day before she was transferred to rehab. The same as two previous visits he had made, Fancy tagged along. While he visited Rianna, Fancy shopped. Afterwards, on the way back to Memphis they would usually stop to have lunch or dinner before getting on the highway.

Rianna's recovery was going pretty good despite her having been labeled by the staff a *diva* and *drama queen.* She craved and demanded almost constant attention from the staff, including the nurses and doctors. Nothing was to her satisfaction. The therapists, if one asked Rianna, did not know what they were doing. She could not understand how any of them got jobs there. Her culinary demands were such that no one put up a fuss when food deliveries ordered by her were made to the facility several times a week.

She was a tough patient, to say the least, and eager to get out of rehab. She worked hard with the so-called incompetent staff, and after being in rehab exactly 22 days, she was discharged.

Stiles agreed to pick her up. This time he came alone. No way was he taking a chance with upsetting Rianna by bringing Fancy with him.

Rianna's speech had improved dramatically, but she still had difficulty walking. Her facial injuries looked much better, although she still had noticeable swelling. The wiring had been removed from her fractured jawbone and she was able to start eating more solid foods, which was welcomed by her after being fed through an IV or having liquid foods only. There was a deep scar on her left cheek that traveled like a crooked road from her lower cheek up to her temple. Her ankles and wrist were still braced.

The two and a half hour ride with Rianna from Nashville to Memphis was relatively quiet. Music from the radio was the only thing that got Stiles through the awkward drive.

When he was on the last stretch leading into the city, he asked Rianna, “Where do you want me to take you?”

She eyed him like he had just cussed her out. “Where do you think I’m going? Home, of course,” she said, stuttering when she spoke. “My best friend Tiny is supposed to meet us outside the gate. She’s going to spend a few days with me. The nurse is supposed to come tomorrow,” she added.

“That’s good.”

“I don’t think I’ll be needing them for too long. I can get around in the wheelchair. That’s one thing I can say I learned, how to maneuver while I was in that horrible dungeon of a place,” she complained.

“You’ll be back to normal sooner than you think.” Stiles ignored her whining. “Look how far you’ve come already. God is good.”

“Humph. Have you heard from your trifling brother?” she barked while Stiles continued driving, relieved to be turning onto Elvis Presley Boulevard.

“Yeah, a couple days ago. He’s concerned about you. He called the hospital as often as he could—considering.”

“Considering? Considering what? That he’s divorcing me and leaving me without a dime after I’ve tried to be a good wife to him? Now that I’ve been in this accident he wants to divorce me? How low can a person go? Who does he think besides me will take care of his affairs while he's locked up?"

Stiles had heard enough. He didn't speak roughly, but remained humble and soft spoken yet stern. "Look, you and I both know that's not how things were before your accident. He hardly ever saw you. You never answered his calls. You spent his money like running water. Come on now, Rianna. You used him and you know it."

"Don't you dare accuse me of using Hezekiah. Okay, so I didn't run up and down that boring highway every week. I sure didn't," she said, wincing and frowning like she was in pain, yet she kept talking. "But I kept money on his books. As far as him calling me, yes I may have missed some of his calls, but that was no reason to have me served divorce papers, and while I was in rehab!"

Stiles didn't know about that latest piece. Hezekiah failed to tell him that, but it did make Stiles feel a bit of satisfaction for his brother. He had a feeling Rianna was going to go for his brother's jugular and try to extract every single remaining penny Hezekiah had. She was going to use this accident as much as possible to her advantage. He hoped his brother, though behind bars, had enough ammunition to make her his ex-wife without her breaking his bank and wrecking his life. That was yet to be seen.

Just as she said, when they pulled up to Lion's Gate, Tiny's beat up car was parked outside the entrance.

Stiles stopped before pulling up to the gate.

"Follow us," he told Tiny when Rianna pointed to where she was parked.

Tiny did as she was told as her car sputtered behind his car.

"Thanks, Stiles," Rianna said when he pulled in the driveway of her and Hezekiah's home.

"I'm going to help you inside. I'm not going to leave you out here to fend for yourself. Give me a little credit."

"No, it's not that."

Tiny jumped out of her car after parking on the street and ran up to Rianna's car door and opened it. She hugged her. "I'm so glad to have you home," she squealed. "Come on, let's get you in the house." She fully opened the car door so Rianna had room to extend her legs out the car.

Looking back over her shoulder, she spoke to Stiles. "Oh, I'm sorry, Pastor," she blushed, "I didn't mean to ignore you. How are you?"

"No worries, Miss Tiny. I'm good. How are you?"

"I'm good," she said shyly.

Stiles retrieved the wheelchair from the trunk and brought it around to Rianna's side.

Tiny skillfully helped her into the wheelchair while Stiles stood to the side with his hand extended so he could help support her.

He remained with the ladies and walked on the opposite of Rianna while Tiny pushed her to the side door where it was a flat surface, making it easier to transport Rianna inside the house.

"Thank you again, Stiles. What do I owe you?"

"Come on, now. You know better. All you owe me is to keep getting better. Call me if you need anything. I'll check on you tomorrow."

"Goodnight, Pastor Graham," Tiny said, batting her long faux minx lashes and smiling. She walked up to the door, positioned her petite body closer than necessary to him, and said, "I've been meaning to tell you how much I enjoy your sermons," she flirted.

"Thank you. I'm glad to hear that. Maybe you'll consider becoming an official member of New Holy Rock since you visit quite often," he noted.

"Uh, sure, I'm thinking about it," she blushed.

"You do that. Goodnight, ladies. Rest well, Rianna." He pulled the door closed.

Tiny leaned against the back of the door. “OMG, that man is *soooo* fine.”

“Girl, please. Stop fantasizing. Help me to my bedroom please, ma’am. You can take any of the two guest rooms. It’s your choice.”

†

“Stiles is a good man. If only I was cut out to be a first lady, I would have married that man,” Victoria confessed to Fancy.

The ladies were having dinner at a Mediterranean restaurant in Horn Lake, Mississippi that they both liked.

“Yes, he sure is. That’s why I’m glad you were honest with him. It would have been a disaster for you and him if you had settled into a long term relationship when you knew you didn’t want that kind of lifestyle,” added Fancy.

Victoria smiled and looked at Fancy, then took a bite of her food. “Talking about good, this food gets better every time we come.”

The friends continued talking, shifting their conversation to Xavier and Pepper.

“Pepper seems happy. She reminds me of the old Pepper. I’m so thankful she got over that postpartum psychosis. That was the most devastating illness I’ve ever had to see, let alone help her deal with it,” Victoria shared.

"I didn't know if she was going to come through, but God showed up and look at her now. Xavier seems happy too. They seem to have a solid marriage," Fancy remarked, popping a piece of buttery bread into her mouth.

"Yes, I believe the fact that they were friends before they got married helps them. I know you don't want to talk about Xavier but—"

"Then let's not. Not in that way. He says he's doing good and that's what I'm going to believe. He is *not* and I do mean *not* going back to the Xavier we both know."

"Okay, okay," Victoria insisted, raising a hand to halt her friend. "I didn't mean anything."

"I know. It's just a sensitive subject for me. I pray for that child every day. I just want things to work out for him and his beautiful little family. Those boys are so precious and Pepper is such a good girl."

"Thank you, Fancy," Victoria said. "I love you."

"I love you too, bestie." They squeezed each other's hands across the table. "Let's have a toast to brighter times ahead."

"Let's do it," Victoria said, smiling, raising her glass.

twenty-four

"Every passing minute is another chance to turn it all around." C. Crowe

Stiles locked his car door and trekked across the street toward the university's campus. He and some of the other online instructors for the university had been summoned for an impromptu in-person staff meeting.

It was seldom that he had to make in-person visits to the campus, which was part of what he liked about online teaching. He could do it pretty much from the leisure of his home, at New Holy Rock, or just about anywhere he had a computer and Wi-Fi, even from his iPhone. Today's technology was always proving to invent things that seemed to keep people apart rather than bringing them together. But such is life, and Stiles rolled with the punches, most of the time.

The mid-morning fall weather was true to the season. It was cool, not cold, but windy and a little overcast. Leaves were blowing in the wind, in their magical shades of reds and golden browns as they skipped about signifying summer was long gone.

He walked swiftly toward Haas Faculty Building. His eyes zeroed in on the text message that popped up as he went about his way.

"Excuse me. Sir, excuse me."

Stiles looked up and stopped in his tracks when he saw the most attractive woman he'd seen in a very long time.

Short curly locks of golden hair perfectly framed her moon-shaped face the color of brown sugar with a pop of fire red polished lips.

His words caught in his throat. "Ye...yes," he said, hoping he didn't sound like a foolish young school kid talking to his school crush for the first time.

"I was wondering if you could tell me where Haas Faculty Building is located. I'm not good at reading this campus map. This place is huge and this is my first time, no actually my second time, that I've been on campus. My first time having to find the Haas Building," she nervously explained.

"No problem, it's straight ahead on the other side of that building over there," he explained, pointing. "I'm headed that way. You're welcome to walk with me," he offered.

She hesitated, and then said, "Sure." They began walking and Stiles suddenly stopped walking. So did she, looking at Stiles curiously.

"I'm sorry, I didn't introduce myself. My name is Stiles...Stiles Graham. I'm one of the university's online instructors."

"Nice to meet you, Stiles. My name is Mya Dugard. I'm an online Statistics instructor." She laughed nervously. "This is my first time doing remote teaching. I hope I made the right decision," she said as she started walking with Stiles next to her. "Have you been doing this a long time?"

"Going on five years. My main occupation is that of associate pastor. I do this because I enjoy teaching but I didn't want to be confined to a classroom. Teaching remotely allows me to dedicate the time and attention I need to my ministry and teach too. It's like having the best of both worlds."

"Good for you."

"What about you?" Stiles asked while they continued strolling.

"I moved to Memphis from California last year when my stepmother got sick. My father and stepmother moved here eight years ago. My father died a couple of years ago and my stepmother died last year. I haven't made up my mind if I want to go back to California or stay here."

"I see," remarked Stiles, finding her both interesting and attractive.

"My son's father lives here so that's another reason I've hung around. For my son's sake, not mine," she clarified. "So until I make up my mind I decided I'd try my hand at remote teaching. I taught middle school in California. This is my first time teaching college age young adults. I hope I can handle it."

"Oh, you'll do fine. It's a piece of cake. Once you have your lesson plan in place all you have to do is dispense the assignments and wait on them to send them in at the designated time."

"You make it sound easy," she said, flashing a perfect smile that made Stiles nervous.

He opened the door as they approached the building. "Here we go," he said, extending his hand for her to step inside.

"Thank you. Wow, this place is huge and it has so much history," she acknowledged as they traipsed up the extravagant hallways full of pictures and historical data lining the towering walls of the institution.

"Yes, this is a beautiful campus. Most of the buildings have a historical charm to them. The newer buildings aren't like this but I think they're still gorgeous. I always enjoy myself when I *do* have to come on campus. I usually take a self-guided tour. That way I can take my time and see what's new around campus. Well, here we are," he said.

Mya looked above the door and read the words aloud. FACULTY ROOM 7. She looked at her phone. “Yep, Room 7. This is it.”

Again, Stiles behaved like the gentleman he was and opened the door for her to go in. Several other instructors already present greeted the couple as they entered.

The meeting began at its designated time. By the time it ended, it was two o’clock in the afternoon.

They walked out of the building together, chatting about the changes being made with remote learning.

“Thanks again for showing me around and sticking by me during the meeting. I see I have a lot to learn and get used to, like logging into the system within the allotted time, entering my lesson plans, online grading, learning how to interact with my students virtually.”

“Believe me, once you do it a few times, you’ll be able to do it blindfolded. I promise,” Stiles teased and chuckled. “If you have trouble, remember you’ve got me to help,” he lightly flirted.

“Well, this is my chariot,” she said, stopping and standing in front of a late modeled ash gray Nissan Sentra.

“Okay, it was nice meeting you.”

“You too, Stiles.” Mya smiled and walked up to her car door.

"Hey, if you don't mind me asking, do you have a church home?"

"Oh, that's right. You did say you were a pastor. No, not officially. I've still been going to the church my father and stepmother were members of before they passed. But to be honest with you, I don't see myself becoming a member. I don't want to sound critical, but it's one of those small churches where the members are mostly senior citizens and related to each other. I mean I'm no spring chicken myself, but I still want to fellowship with people I can relate to. Someone my age or where there are ministries and things to do. Know what I mean?"

"I do know what you mean and that's understandable."

"Some Sundays I visit different churches, but I'm a forty-three year old woman with a teenage son, I don't want to age myself too quickly but I don't want to be somewhere that I come off as a teeny bopper either. I want to belong to a church where I feel comfortable and a church where my son can meet friends and be in a positive faith-based environment. So, usually if we don't find a church we both want to visit we'll end up staying at home and watching church on television. It's not the same though."

"In that case I would like to invite you and your son, without pressure," he said, flashing a charming smile, "to visit New Holy Rock. The congregation is quite diverse with an equal mixture of high school, college age, people our age, all the way to senior citizens. We branched off from a larger church a couple of years ago so we're still growing, but I think you would feel comfortable there and so will your son. "Here," Stiles reached inside his jacket pocket and pulled out a business card and passed it to her. "Here you go. This is my personal card. It has my cell number as well as the church's information. I'd love to see you sitting in the sanctuary Sunday or maybe during our mid-week service. Again, I'm not pressuring you. Just wanted to invite you and let you know you'd be welcomed with open arms." Was he coming off like he was flirting? He hoped not, then again why wouldn't he; she was beautiful.

Mya smiled, almost blushed, and looked at the card. "Sure, thank you, *Pastor* Graham. Let me call the number now. That way you can have my number too. I mean, well just in case..." she paused and blushed.

"Perfect."

She dialed the number on the card. Seconds later his phone started ringing. He looked at his screen, looked at her, and then smiled. "Saved," he said, grinning, "Oh, and feel free to use that number if you get hung up on the online teaching thing. Like I said, it takes some getting used to, but you'll get the hang of it, but if you don't, give me a call." He flashed another captivating smile.

"Ok, thanks." Mya extended her hand to open her car door.

Stiles stepped up and opened it, holding it back until she got inside.

"Thanks...again."

"My pleasure. Drive carefully."

She started the car as Stiles walked away. Resting her head against the head rest, she giggled. Before backing out of the parking space, she studied the business card one last time before sticking it inside her purse and driving away.

twenty-five

"The wages of sin is alimony." Carolyn Wells

Early Tuesday morning, Trevor Price made the trip to visit his client and give him the news about the power of attorney and his impending divorce.

Inside the dark, damp, stale smelling visiting room, Hezekiah was led in handcuffs at his wrists and ankles. He shuffled toward the four by four table.

"Can you remove the handcuffs, at least until he signs these papers?" Trevor asked the guard, pointing to the folder of papers he had.

The guard answered by walking back toward Hezekiah and removing one hand out of the cuffs. He gave Trevor a fixed, emotionless glare before turning and ambling out of the confined space and posting himself outside the locked door.

"She wants alimony for the next seven years unless she remarries before then. In the event of her remarrying, you would no longer have to pay her a cent."

"I want to counter that. We've only been married two years. That's the most time I should have to pay her, that is, if I have to pay anything."

"Okay, sounds reasonable. I'll make that change and present it to her attorney."

"What else?" Hezekiah asked, his patience already wearing thin. He wished he could get up and sling the chair across the room. That would only get him more time in this dump so he restrained himself from acting on that impulsive thought.

"She wants you to pay her attorney fees plus any out of pocket medical expenses related to her accident, *aaand* maintain health insurance on her."

"Can she get what she's asking?"

"More than likely, especially considering right now she's disabled so to speak. What you have going for you believe it or not is the fact you are incarcerated. You don't earn a salary or have a steady income. Yes, you get a stipend from New Holy Rock, but Xavier has assured me that it is not a substantial amount."

"That's my boy," Hezekiah boasted proudly hearing Xavier was looking out for his best interests. Xavier may not have made but one trip up the highway to see him, but he had supported him in any way he could from the outside. That meant more than a visit from across a steel prison table.

He hadn't talked to his eldest son, but at least that meant they weren't at each other's throats. Plus, Stiles had assured him on more than one occasion that Khalil's attitude seemed to be softening when he talked about him. Maybe that was because he was now a father himself. Parenthood could do that. It could soften the toughest heart.

"So, here you go. The papers declaring me Power of Attorney. From this point forward and until you make the change, I have the power and authority to act as you and on your behalf. Anything your wife—"

"Soon to be *ex*-wife," Hezekiah interjected.

"Anything your *ex*-wife wants or needs," Trevor explained, "she'll have to come through me. She received her last payment from New Holy Rock this past Monday. Any and all access or authority to use your credit cards has been terminated. All locks are changed so she will not be able to freely come and go in and out of New Holy Rock. Her office has been cleared out and her personal things were packed. Your brother is going to see to her getting the items she left. Oh, yeah, she did ask for two credit cards with no less than a $5,000 limit on each with her as the authorized user. You, of course would be the responsible party to pay the debt."

Hezekiah laughed nervously. “That accident must have left her missing a few marbles. She’s run up the ones she had almost to the max. I won’t give her another dime. Not if I can help it.”

“Maybe this will make you feel better. She has also been officially relieved of her position as Minister of Music, and the request that she be appointed interim senior pastor was unequivocally denied by the board.”

“She’s ludicrous for even thinking that would ever happen,” Hezekiah lashed out.

Trevor continued, “Upon her being served with these papers, which she has agreed to receive through her attorney, the both of you will be declared legally single while we work through the finalities of the divorce. But I don’t expect her to contest.”

“I may be behind bars, but I’m still going to do everything in my power to stop her from ruining the rest of my life.”

“I believe her lawyer will advise her client that this is a darn good deal. Especially in light that you have no minor children, no joint property, and you’ve only been married two years.”

“You don’t know Rianna. It’s not always that simple with her.”

“We’ll see,” said Trevor. “Do you have any questions?”

"No, I'm good."

"Okay, in that case let me get out of here. I need to make that drive back to Memphis. I have a dinner meeting later this evening. In the meantime I'll get these papers to Rianna's attorney and I'll be going to your bank this week to give them the POA papers. From now on, you can let people know that I'm your POA and feel free to give them my contact information."

"Thanks, Trevor."

"You're welcome. And speaking of thanking me, my fees will continue to be paid by New Holy Rock?"

"Yes, that's right. No worries."

"Well, unless you have something else you want to discuss, I'll be on my way. Take care of yourself, Hezekiah. Until next time."

"Will do. Oh, one more thing,"

"What's that?" Trevor asked.

"Did you hear about my criminal case lawyer?"

"No, what about him?"

"He had to step away from his practice due to illness. A new fellow joined the firm. He's going to represent my criminal charges. I'm counting on him to get me an appeal, new trial, or do whatever to get me out of here."

"You know his name? I'll check him out."

"I've done that already, but you can still see what you can find out. Name's Christian Black. S'posed to be some big shot lawyer out of New York."

"Gotcha. I'll get back with you. Call me when you can. I'll be back in two weeks unless something comes up before then. Good evening, Reverend." Trevor stood up, pushing back the chair with the back of his thighs. He leaned forward and reached across the table to shake Hezekiah's hand.

Trevor departed and Hezekiah shuffled back to his cell with his spirit uplifted. Trevor Price's visit had done the trick. All seemed to be going well.

On his bunk, Hezekiah prayed to himself. Thanking God for all he was doing in his life. He prayed the next thing would be for God to get him out of this hell hole. Until then he would keep holding Sunday service and keep his mind on a positive note.

After he prayed, he retrieved his cell phone. He wondered what Fancy was up to. He wanted to hear her voice. He'd called her phone a couple of times as an UNKNOWN CALLER but he always ended the call before she answered. He didn't call her although he wanted to stay in touch, but he told himself it wouldn't be fair to her. He was not only in prison but he was married to another woman.

He was not going to mess with her head or her life. However, tonight the urge was strong. He replayed mental visions of when they spent the night at her hotel. It was like something out of a fairytale. He missed her so much. Now that he knew he was closer to getting a divorce, maybe Fancy would at least talk to him for a few minutes.

He sighed and then dialed her number again. The phone rang several times. No answer. "That's my sign," he said, "to leave things the way they are." He turned off his phone and returned it to its hiding place.

†

Fancy ran to the bathroom where she'd mistakenly left her phone. It stopped ringing as soon as she stepped foot in the bathroom. She picked it up and looked at the screen. UNKNOWN CALLER. "Umm." She shrugged and returned to the living room where she and Sebastian had been curled on the sofa. She picked up the novel she was reading, read a few lines, and then placed it on the arm of the sofa, laid her head against the fluffy sofa pillow and closed her eyes. Her last thought before drifting off to sleep was about of all people—Hezekiah.

twenty-six

"If there's even a slight chance at getting something that will make you happy, risk it. Life's too short and happiness is too rare."
A. Lucas

Stiles toyed around aimlessly on his MacBook, his mind all over the place instead of on the pop quiz he was supposed to be uploading for his students.

Sitting in his home office, without prompting of any kind, he smiled as he replayed his encounter with Mya Dugard the week before. He picked up his phone from next to his MacBook, pulled up his CONTACTS, and scrolled until he came to her name and number.

Before he had time to think about what he was about to do, he pressed the CALL button. To his surprise the phone started ringing right away. He looked at the screen to be certain it was her number he had dialed—it was.

"Well....*hellooo*, Pastor Graham," a cheery voice answered.

He smiled at the thought that she had saved his number and addressed him by his formal name.

"Okay, since you want to go there with the formalities. Let me say it again. Hello, *Miz* Dugard." Stiles chuckled.

He heard her giggle into the phone and that made his heart glad.

"I stand corrected...*Stiles*. You got me," Mya replied, laughing.

"That's better," he said. "I hope I didn't catch you at a bad time."

"No, actually this is a perfect time. I'm just relaxing until I decide what I'm going to have for dinner later. How are you and to what do I owe the pleasure of this call?"

Her voice was light, welcoming and exciting, endearing her to him even more. "I wanted to see how things were going with remote teaching. Are you getting used to uploading your lessons and quizzes?"

"Yes, you were right; after I practiced uploading a few lessons, I haven't had any problems."

"Cool," Stiles paused, "uh, you said you were trying to decide what you were having for dinner?"

"Yes, I usually eat a big lunch and a light dinner, but today I skipped lunch altogether. When I did go out, I planned to stop and pick up something, but I was lazy and came home instead," Mya easily said. "My son is spending the weekend with his dad. He gets him from school every other Thursday and he's with him until Sunday so I have time to do me. This usually consists of me eating takeout and watching Netflix." She laughed.

"Is that right. Well, I was calling to invite you to have dinner with me tomorrow evening, but since you haven't eaten yet, we can do it tonight. My schedule is flexible."

"Ohhh, that's a nice gesture," she said softly almost with a little reserve in her voice.

"I understand if you have other plans. I'm sure a single attractive lady like you has no shortage of dinner invitations," he purposely flirted.

"You got jokes, huh?" she countered. "Seriously, I don't date often. I should say I don't date at all. At least I haven't since my divorce."

"If you don't mind me asking, how long ago was your divorce?"

"Four years ago."

"Wow, that's a long time to be alone."

"I don't look at it like that. Before my mom and stepdad died, I was their caregiver so that took up a majority of my free time. They're no longer here, but my son keeps me busy. Between his school, running track, and playing football, my schedule stays full. I hardly have time for myself, let alone date, even if I wanted to."

"I understand, but you still need to take time for yourself."

"I guess you're right. But what about you? Your dating life must be interesting with you being a single pastor and all."

"I was seeing someone, but that ended months ago."

"Oh, I see."

"Being a pastor isn't always the ideal occupation. A lot of ladies don't want someone who works for the Lord." He chuckled. "It takes someone who can dedicate themselves to the ministry and who understands my busy schedule."

"Sounds like we have something in common," Mya said.

"Oh, so you're a pastor too," Stiles joked.

"No way, but I do keep a very tight schedule. Until my son leaves for college in a few years, I dedicate as much time to him as possible. Speaking of children, do you have kids?"

Stiles was quiet.

"Hello? You still there?"

"Ye...yes. And no, I don't have children. Well, let me rephrase that. I had a little girl, Audrey was her name."

"Did you say *was* her name?" questioned Mya. "What does that mean?"

"She..." he spoke with deliberate caution, "was killed in a car accident some years ago."

"My God, I'm so sorry," she apologized, wishing she hadn't brought up children.

"It's okay. I'm all right. So, what about dinner?" Toning down the tenseness of the conversation.

"You know what; I think I'd like that. It'll be good to break my routine."

"Okay." Stiles was elated. "Tonight or tomorrow?"

"Tonight's good."

"Okay, six-thirty?"

"Six-thirty's perfect. Where should I meet you?" She wasn't ready to tell him where she lived. It was far too early to even think about that.

"Uh, I can pick you up unless you prefer to meet me. It's on you."

"I'll meet you," she said.

"Okay, anyplace in particular where you'd like to eat?"

"No, not really. I'm not a picky eater so just about any place is good for me. I live in midtown, if that helps."

"Okay, let's see. Midtown?" he said aloud. "What about Sage Restaurant on Main. Have you eaten there before?"

"Yes, my son and I have eaten there several times. He loves their strawberry cheesecake French toast. And me, I've never had anything as good as their Japanese fried chicken sandwich. I'm telling you, it's to die for," Mya chimed. "Oh, my lord, I'm making myself hungry."

"Don't worry, when we get there I'll let you order *all* you want." He laughed. "I'll see you later."

†

Dinner was divine. Mya and Stiles easily talked, laughed, and got along quite well. In some ways, her light and bubbly personality reminded him of Rena.

He hadn't gone out on a date since Victoria ended things. It felt good to have the company of someone of the opposite sex that wasn't business or church related.

"Thanks for letting me eat all I wanted," Mya said, laughing and patting her tummy as they left out of the restaurant. "I'm full as a tick."

"Good for you, and boy am I glad I ordered that strawberry cheesecake French toast. I see why it's your son's favorite. It was spot on."

"I told you," Mya replied, blushing.

"*Soooo*, we'll have to do this again," Stiles suggested as he walked her to her car.

"I'd like that."

"Tomorrow night too soon?" he boldly asked. "Remember, I initially invited you to have dinner with me tonight *or* tomorrow."

"And I chose tonight," she said, batting her natural eyelashes.

"Are you against eating with me two nights in a row, Mya?" he looked at her intensely as they stood next to her car in the moonlit parking lot.

"No, of course not. But I don't want to wear out my welcome," she said softly, looking away briefly before looking back up at him.

The attraction they had for each other was obvious as they stared into each other's eyes. It was quite a cool evening, on the verge of being chilly. He could easily see himself wrapping her inside the warmth and protection of his arms. He wanted so badly to pull her into his arms and kiss her, but being the gentleman he was he didn't want to come off as being overly aggressive. After all, they were just getting to know each other and he didn't want to make her uncomfortable in any way.

"Sure, why not?" Mya answered with a smile.

"Great," he said, a huge grin appearing on his handsome, freshly shaved face as they stared momentarily at each other—again.

He broke the enticing moment by opening her car door and allowing her to get inside. Closing the door when he was sure she was seated, he bid her goodbye and stood watching her until she drove off before he went and got in his car.

On his way home, he called Fancy and told her about his date.

"I'm so happy for you. It's about time you took the plunge again and started back dating. And you say she's a teacher. Y'all have something in common already. That's good. When are you going to see her again?"

"We're going to dinner again tomorrow night."

"Tell me more about her," Fancy urged.

"Well, she's divorced, has a teenage son. Very attractive and a great sense of humor. She's originally from California. Her parents were living here, but they both passed away within a couple of years of each other. She hasn't decided whether or not she'll move back to California, but so far she said she doesn't have plans to. Her son has made friends and a life here and his father lives here. She doesn't want to disrupt that. Overall, she seems like a nice girl. She was easy to talk to. We laughed all during dinner."

"What about her faith? Is she a believer or what?"

"Yes, but she isn't a member of any church here. Before her folks died, she and her son were going to their church, but she's looking for a church home for the two of them."

"Did you invite her to New Holy Rock?"

"You know it. She seemed receptive, but I didn't push her. If she comes it'll have to be her choice. I'll find out some more about her when we have dinner tomorrow evening. I just wanted to let you know that I'm back in business." Stiles laughed and so did Fancy.

"Good for you. If anyone deserves a good woman and someone to love, it's you."

"Why, thank you, Fancy. That means a lot to me."

"Boy, please, I tell you that all the time. Anyway, I'm going to let you go. I'm working on some designs for a new client."

"Oh, cool. By the way, how's the interior design business coming along? Being your own boss, setting your own hours..."

"Good, but I told you even though I love it, I still don't want to do it full time, only at my leisure."

"I need to get you over to my crib so you can add some of your special touches to spruce it up."

"Gladly, 'cause that place can use a little sprucing up. It looks like a straight up old single man's place with all those brown and beige colors. You need some light and bold colors in your life," Fancy said, chuckling at what she'd said.

The next few minutes as Stiles neared his home, they kept talking.

"I wanted to tell you that I plan to go see Hezekiah Tuesday. He called the other day. Said everything was going smoothly and that Trevor Price took care of filing for his divorce and finalizing the POA papers. He should be all set."

"Thank you, God!" Fancy said, almost shouting over the phone. "I know he has to be happy about that. What about Rianna. Have you heard from her? I wonder how she's doing since the accident."

"I talked to her yesterday. I went to see her last week and she looked like she was on the road to a full recovery. She's still in a wheelchair. She said she still has to be careful about putting weight on her ankles. The doctor told her to stay off of her feet for another three weeks. She's still upset about the facial scarring, but she said the plastic surgeon told her he was going to do what he could to hide as much scarring as possible. It's more than likely going to require several surgeries."

"I hate to say it, but at least this accident has kept her quiet. She can't run around stirring up a bunch of mess and confusion wherever she goes. But I still send up prayers on her behalf. It's the least I can do."

"You're a good woman, Fancy. A mighty good woman. My brother was a fool to treat you the way he did, but I have a feeling sitting up in a cell that he's thought about that. I know he loves you."

"You keep telling me that and I don't know why," said Fancy.

"'Cause you know I'm speaking the truth. If and when he gets released, I have a feeling he's going to run back to you."

"Thing about that is, I don't know if I'll let him back in. I didn't tell you this, but we slept together, me and Hezekiah. It was before he married Rianna and before he got shot."

"Why am I not surprised?" Stiles replied. "You just proved my point. You wouldn't and you don't just sleep with anybody. You're not that type of woman so that proves your true feelings. He loves you. You love him."

"If you say so...if you say so," Fancy repeated. "Hey, I almost forgot."

"What's that?" said Stiles.

"I'm having a small family dinner next Sunday for Xavier's twenty-fifth birthday. I'm going to have all his favorite foods."

"When is his actual birthday?"

"It's the following Monday. I'm telling you a week ahead of time, so no excuses; I expect you to be there."

"What time?"

"Three-thirty. That should give everyone time to get done churching. And you already know you're expected because you're family. You're Xavier's uncle. I guess you can say you'll be standing in for his father."

"In that case, I wouldn't miss it for the world."

"Oh, and heads up, Victoria's coming. I hope you don't mind."

"Of course I don't mind. Why would I? It'll be good to see her."

"Okay, cool. You can bring your new lady friend if you'd like."

"Whoa, it's not like that. I just met the woman."

"Okay. Suit yourself. I was just letting you know I have no qualms about it. And just because you say she's not your lady *now*, I have a feeling it won't be long before that relationship status gets upgraded."

"Ha, ha, ha. You got jokes," Stiles said.

twenty-seven

"Your words mean nothing when your actions are the complete opposite."
IHearts143Quotes

"Happy birthday to ya, happy birthday to ya," the group of family and friends song in the tune of Stevie Wonder's hit birthday song while holding raised crystal glasses of champagne and sparkling apple cider for those who didn't prefer alcohol.

At the end of the rendition, Khalil sang, raising his glass of champagne "*And many mooore...* Cheers, li'l brother. May this be your best birthday ever and may you be blessed to enjoy many more in the years to come. I'm proud to call you my brother. I love you, man."

The guests raised their glasses in unison with Khalil. Fancy and Victoria discreetly wiped tears from their eyes over Khalil's touching tribute.

The brothers hadn't always seen eye to eye, but marriage, wives, having kids, and the pure trials of life had brought them closer than ever. Their wives got along and Pepper considered Eliana more than just a sister-in-law; she looked at her as a real friend and Eliana felt the same.

Fancy watched with pride as Xavier blew out the candles and cut the first slice of the multi-tiered red velvet cake with butter cream frosting and roasted pecans on top—his favorite.

†

Around the corner from Fancy's house, Rianna lay in her bed, sulking and feeling sorry for herself. Abel hadn't called, and he never responded or replied to the text his wife had sent Rianna of Abel, her and their darling little family. She was taken by total surprise when she saw the picture of Abel cuddling a newborn baby with his other arm wrapped around his wife.

"Dang," she muttered. "You could have at least had the decency to tell me you got your wife knocked up."

It wasn't that she was so disturbed that he'd made a baby with his wife, that wasn't the real issue. She was perturbed because Abel turned out to be like all the other scoundrels she'd dated or fooled around with. He got what he wanted from her, when he wanted it, and in return all she got was a few lousy dollars and expensive gifts and trips, maybe good sex every now and then. She was approaching the doorway to forty. Life seemed to be passing her by in a way she hadn't expected.

She thought life with Hezekiah would be different. Her dreams of being a First Lady had been fulfilled but it was far from being like the life she'd dreamed about. The first lady's life seemed to be glorious, happy, and a role people loved and respected. Unlike the life she was presently living. Her heavy heart sank deeper at the situation she was in. The accident, her scarred face, and the possibility she would have a limp the rest of her life was keeping her in a deep depressive state.

Hezekiah, needless to say, was no more than a villain himself in Godly clothing. She liked him, but she never loved him. How could she when she knew he was using her and vice versa. She was nobody's fool—she knew Hezekiah was still in love with Fancy.

"God, will I ever find a love of my own? Don't you have someone out there who will love me for me? Who'll treat me like a queen and look at me with love and lust in their eyes. Why can't I have that? Is that too much to ask? And what about my face?" She sat up in the bed and cried into her hands as she pleaded with God then grabbed her phone and looked at herself. "Look at me! Why did you do this to *meeee*!" She wept.

Crying uncontrollably for several minutes, she stopped and started wiping away her tears and snotty nose with the back of her hand before leaning over and getting a hand towel off the night stand next to her bed. She wiped her face again, and then looked at the papers lying on the bed next to her. She picked them up and began reading the document which her lawyer had delivered this past Friday. It was now Sunday evening and this was the first time she gave attention to the packet. Going over the stipulations and demands their lawyers had discussed, there was one thing she hadn't agreed on but she ended up losing anyway. That was that she was not going to be able to remain in this house. She looked around the bedroom. She hadn't spent nearly as much time in Lion's Gate as she had initially anticipated like she thought being the wife of someone as well known and financially stable as Hezekiah McCoy. Yet, this room, with all its fancy furnishings and everything a girl could ask for was soon going to be a thing of the past. Part of the divorce settlement was she had to move out of Lion's Gate. Hezekiah had pulled a slick move. The house was in the name of New Holy Rock and was listed as a PARSONAGE. Now that she was no longer going to be First Lady, she could not remain in the home. She would be moving back to Apartment

3D in the days coming up. She wiped away a fresh batch of tears.

Clicking the ink pen to extend its tip, she studied the document again and then sighing heavily and with tears continually flowing, she signed on the dotted line.

Her doorbell rang just as she'd finished signing her name. "Must be Tiny," she mumbled.

Minutes later, Tiny appeared at the entrance to Rianna's bedroom.

"I used my key," Tiny said, holding the spare key Rianna had given her up in the air. "Girl, what's going on around the corner? You know I always get lost coming inside this community. I ended up on Fancy's street. I saw a bunch of cars in her driveway and lined up and down both sides of the street.

"I…I don't know," Rianna said sounding sad.

Seeing her friend was crying, she rushed over to the bed. "What's wrong?"

"Nothing. I'm good," Rianna answered.

"Girl, please. You know I know you. You are not sitting up in the middle of the bed cryin' for nothing." Tiny turned and looked at the big screen television posted on the wall in front of Rianna's king-sized bed.

"The TV ain't on so you can't say you was looking at one of those sad movies. Talk to me." Tiny paused when she paid attention to the papers Rianna still held in one hand.

"Hol' up..." she eased the papers out of Rianna's hand, glanced at the words, saw Rianna's signature, and then faced her friend. "I'm so sorry, Rianna."

"It's all good, Tiny. It was good while it lasted. Now back to Apartment 3D. Having to go back can't be all that bad. Can it?" Rianna eyed her friend, wiped the last of her tears away, and then went silent.

Tiny sat on the bed and reached for her friend, embracing her in a tight hug. "Nah, it won't be bad, not at all. Sometimes we hafta go back before we can move ahead. But if anybody can move ahead from this, it's you, Rianna."

"I hope you're right, Tiny. I hope you're right."

twenty-eight

"There is no greater agony than bearing an untold story inside you." Maya Angelou

It was another depressing Monday morning; a repeat of how he'd spent the last 533 days and nights behind filthy, stinking, violent prison walls. Hezekiah watched national news on the television that hung on the concrete wall in the common area of the prison.

MSNBC showed a clip of the president stumbling up the lawn of the White House, unknowingly walking in the wrong direction and seemingly ignoring or not hearing the agents steering him in the right direction. Hezekiah laughed and so did some of the other inmates watching the clip.

The local news came on following the end of MSNBC news. Hezekiah rose from the steel chair he was seated in, ready to go back to his cell. He stopped suddenly and focused on the screen again when he heard the name of Jude's stepfather—Vernon Clay. It was a quick clip but the journalist said the suspect had waived his rights to a jury trial and accepted a plea deal to shooting Pastor Hezekiah McCoy of

New Holy Rock. It seems he was upset about being outed as a sexual offender by McCoy and was set on revenge. He pleaded guilty and the judge sentenced him to seven years."

Hezekiah bit on his bottom lip and walked out of the common area, back to his cell. "Seven freaking years? That's it? For attempted murder? And I'm sitting in this dungeon for twenty? Heck, nah..."

When he got back to his cell, he called Mariah from his cell phone. No answer. He ended the call and put the phone back in its safety place, but he was still upset that Jude's stepfather had gotten off with a slap on the wrist. Life certainly was unfair.

†

The same Monday morning, in the suburb of Collierville, Christian and Luna were getting ready for work. The home they'd chosen to rent for the time being met all their needs. The five bedrooms, five and a half bathrooms, 4100 square feet home was representative of Luna's high dollar taste. She was accustomed to having nice and expensive things, and marrying a man like Christianaldo who shared in her vision and drive made their relationship as close to perfection as perfection could get in a relationship.

"Honey, do you want me to check with you around lunch time and see if we can meet somewhere close to both of our offices?" Christian asked while standing in front of the floor length mirror to check himself. The black Italian two-buttoned, two-piece suit fit his five-eleven frame and thick muscular calves and thighs like it had been especially tailored for him. He was by no means a man with a six-pack. But he looked good, had a nicely shaped close cut beard, close haircut, smooth chocolate melanin skin, and he always smelled good.

Luna, just as stylish and sharply dressed as her husband, chose a fuchsia plus size Alexander McQueen single-breasted two button blazer with black straight leg pants. The tailor fit of the blazer showed off her narrow waist. Though she was a thick woman, she had curves in all the right places.

They were wise when it came to their finances but neither of them hesitated to treat each other well and to treat themselves well. They believed in indulging in the finer things of life such as going on exotic vacations to places near and far, enjoying the best of cuisines, and staying at five star hotels. They didn't squander their money; they budgeted more than enough money to enjoy life to the fullest—together.

Children had not been in the cards for the otherwise happy, successful couple. It was not because they did not want children. Christian, when he was a young kid, was riding on the back of his friend's bicycle when after hitting a sharp curve, he was thrown off the bike, sustaining a serious injury to his testicles and causing sterility. The couple had discussed adoption many times, but they agreed to put off adoption until they were ready to settle down and commit to raising kids.

"Meeting for lunch sounds good, babe." Luna picked up her purse and tablet from off the night table and they headed down the stairs out the door to their respective vehicles.

Christian came back around to where his wife stood, opened her car door, gathered her thickness into his arms before she got inside the car, and kissed her like they were newlyweds. All the years they'd been together and he still could never get enough of her. He sucked in the sweet scent of her hair and the tantalizing fragrance of her perfume and instantly became excited.

"Christian," she moaned and felt herself becoming aroused as well. "You *would* wait until it's time for us to leave," she whispered as their lips slowly parted.

"It gives us something to look forward to tonight. Right?" he said.

"I can't wait," said Luna, and she got inside the car. She turned the ignition and let the window down. "Or maybe we can enjoy a *special* lunch." She laughed seductively, pressed the remote button for the garage, and then backed out, still smiling.

†

Christian mouthed a prayer of gratitude as he headed to the law office. Since relocating to Memphis he rarely if ever had to drive his personal vehicle, a chalk gray Porsche 911 Carrera 4 Cabriolet. Rather, as an added perk from the law firm, he was presented with a leased company car, an oyster pearl Acura RDX.

"Welcome to Brachman Law Firm," the partners and staff greeted Christian when he arrived. A special breakfast buffet had been catered into the office. Danish, Fruit, coffee, tea, bottled water, and an array of fresh hot breakfast sandwiches were part of the spread.

"Thank you," Christian replied. "It's a pleasure to be here and to be part of this upstanding law firm. I'm honored and I feel extremely blessed. My parents, may they both rest in peace, instilled Godly values and morals in me. My mother was an educator, an elementary school teacher. My father, though I was not his biological son, treated me like I was his flesh and blood. He adopted me when I was three years old. God rest his soul. He was a Chicago criminal defense lawyer who believed in the fair treatment and representation of all, but especially people of color who he believed were often unfairly treated. He was a man of faith who practiced his convictions and offered his services to those less fortunate. So cheers to my parents and their teaching. I look forward to us winning cases and keeping this as the number one firm in this city. If I could be half the man he was, I will feel honored and privileged. Again, thank you for having me. Let's go and do the darn thing!"

A roaring round of applause and well wishes rang throughout the firm. After fellowshipping with his peers, he was shown his office with a massive view of downtown Memphis and the mighty Mississippi River.

Alone in his office, he began reminiscing about his life but particularly about his mother and their rocky relationship. What he purposely did not share with people, other than Luna, was that his relationship with his mother had been strained, to say the least, for many years preceding her death. Thank God he was able to forgive her and repair their relationship before she went to glory. It had been devastating for him when his mother, after allowing him to believe the man he knew as his biological father, was not his biological father.

He still remembered that day clearly. Everything about his life up to that point in time, he looked at as a lie. Christian was eighteen at the time, and at home on winter break from college. Just months before, his father Charles, or the man he knew as his father, had been run down and killed by a drunk driver.

His mother and Christian were in the family room watching an episode of one of the top reality DNA cable shows." The young man on the show was there for a DNA test because his mother told him she had lied about who his real father was.

"How could a mother do something like that? That's horrible to grow up believing one thing and then finding out it was all a lie," Christianaldo told his mother, very upset when he heard how it had affected the young man's life.

"I did it," she spurted.

"You did what?"

"I lied....just like that boy's mother."

"What are you talking about, Mama?" asked Christianaldo, turning the volume down so he could hear his mother clearly.

"Honey, what I'm trying to tell you is that Charles was not your biological father."

"What? Is this some kind of a prank?" Christian screamed.

"I wish." His mother started crying. "But it's not. I was fifteen years old. I didn't know a thing about sex, except from what I had heard some of the more popular girls say. I don't know why I did what I did. I had met this really cute boy at school named Franklin who said he liked me. I never had any boy tell me he liked me so you can imagine how special I felt when he said he wanted me to be his girlfriend. He told me we had to keep it a secret because some of the popular girls might get jealous and start bullying me. I skipped my last period class to meet him at his house one afternoon when his momma and daddy wasn't home. We ended up having sex. And yes, it was my first time, but I thought I loved him and he said he loved me, but after the second time we had sex he said he didn't want me to be his girlfriend anymore. I was so hurt.

One Friday, a month after he broke up with me, he came to me after school and invited me to meet him at a party in the projects later than night. I was so excited that he wanted to be with me again. I sneaked out the house and went to the party. He fed me alcohol and we smoked weed, and no, he didn't force me to drink or smoke. Yes, I know we were underage, but I did it because I wanted to fit in. I wanted him to like me again.

I got really really high and drunk that night, and well, I did something shameful. I remember this boy who they called Bae-bruh came in the room while me and Franklin were making out.. Bae-bruh started drinking and smoking with us too. Franklin told me that if I wanted us to get back together I had to prove that I loved him by having sex with Bae-bruh. At first I had said, no, but after drinking and smoking some more, I did it. After that night, Franklin never spoke to me again. He ignored me and acted like I didn't exist. I was devastated. As for Bae-bruh, I never saw him again. I don't even know if he went to our school or not."

"What is wrong with you?" Christian accused. "You were that stupid? You wanted to be liked that much that you slept with some strange guy? Oh, my God!" Christian shook his head in disgust.

"I know, Christian," she cried, "but just listen. Yes, I should have known better to do what I did. I didn't think about the possibility of me getting pregnant; that was the farthest thing from my mind. When I told my momma I had missed my period, she got one of those pregnancy tests. I took it and it came up that I was pregnant. I couldn't tell her who the father

was because I didn't know who he was. Maybe it was Bae-bruh or maybe it was Franklin. All I know is I had had sex with Bae-bruh that night, and not Franklin.

Before I started to show signs of being pregnant, Momma sent me to live with her oldest sister in Tampa, Florida. I never went back to Chicago.

Tampa is where I met Charles at this restaurant I was working at while I was attending college. You were one year old at the time. Me and Charles fell in love. He told me it didn't matter that I had a kid because he would love you like you were his own. And he did, Christian. He was a good man. I never thought a drunk driver would take his life. I miss him every day," his mother cried. "You can be angry with me all you want. I wouldn't blame you, but please don't be mad at Charles. He never asked who your biological father was because he said it didn't matter. And it didn't. I hope you don't think of me as a whore or a slut," she cried. "The good thing about that night is you were conceived. That was a blessing I wouldn't change for anything in this world."

After hearing her story, Christianaldo did not feel empathy for his mother. Instead, the fire of resentment was set ablaze in his heart and he despised her for betraying him.

Over the next six years Christian's contempt for his mother did not waver. He rarely went home during his breaks. It caused a rift in not only the relationship with his mother, but also with the man he regarded as his father.

Ever since his mother told him about his birth father, Christian imagined what kind of person his father was. Did Christian look like him, act like him? Was his father rich, homeless, married with kids? Was he still alive? There had been so many unanswered questions he had to deal with. He used to pray that one day he would find him. Not anymore. As far as he was concerned, Charles Black was the only father who mattered in his life.

Charles did not like the distance between Christian and his mother. He tried to talk to Christian, but it did very little to repair the damage Christian's mother had caused by her withholding the truth from her son and only child. It affected Christian's relationships with women, his way of thinking, and he had a hard time trusting anyone. It sent him spiraling into a dark place when Charles was killed, causing an even wider separation between him and his mother. His perspective changed when his mother fell deathly ill the year after Charles' death.

During that time is when he met Luna. All the apprehension and hesitancy he felt about relationships and women dissipated when Luna entered his life.

Knock. Knock.

The sound of someone knocking pulled him from his thoughts of the past. He swirled around in his brown leather office chair and faced the door. “Come in.”

The door effortlessly swung open.

“Excuse me, Attorney Black.” An attractive older Black woman appearing to be in her mid to late sixties stood at the door stylishly dressed in a navy skirt and blazer ensemble with a white blouse underneath and navy open-toed leather pumps.

“Come in, Miss Agnes. How can I help you?” Miss Agnes, as everyone called her, was his designated law clerk.

Here are the files you asked for. You can find more information on the computer. Did you get your login information?”

“Yes, someone from IT came up when I first got here this morning. They set everything up and gave me my login instructions. I should be good to go.” He stood up and walked around and removed the pile of manila folders out of her hands.

“Thank you for bringing these files. Are there anymore?”

"Maybe a few. I'll check with Beverly. She's your administrative assistant. She may have a couple of files she's still transcribing and entering into the system."

"Don't bother; I'll check with her. Thanks, Miss Agnes."

"You're welcome. My extension is 558. Call me if you need me."

"I sure will, but these should be enough to keep me busy. I need to review these cases thoroughly. Thanks again."

"No problem. And welcome again, Attorney Black."

"Please, call me Christian."

"No problem...*Christian.*" Miss Agnes smiled and exited the office.

Christian meticulously went through the files, paused and picked up one of the thicker file folders. He read the name of the client on the label: *Reverend Hezekiah McCoy.*

twenty-nine

"Man is not what he thinks he is; he is what he hides." André Malraux

Christian, along with his law clerk, made the drive to visit his client, Hezekiah McCoy. Christian had gone through each of the client folders his predecessor left. Hezekiah McCoy was among the most prominent and familiar case, according to the former law partner.

Miss Agnes had the folder lying on her lap as they drove along Highway 40. "Do you have anything in particular you want to bring out during the meeting? I'll take notes before we get there and that way I can make sure we cover everything."

"That's a good idea, Miss Agnes. We already have the things I want to cover in order of importance inside that file. Right?"

"Yes, sir."

"Okay, good. If you haven't already, please add the following: I want to cover some personal things with him and I want to let him know the person responsible for shooting him has started serving his time. He may already know, but I want to mention it just in case he doesn't. I know it has nothing to do with what we're working on for him, but it's something I'm sure he'd like to know. Plus, it'll help us break the ice, get to see what he's all about."

Miss Agnes nodded. She liked her new boss already. She could tell he was a go getter. She could see why he had made such a positive impression with his New York colleagues. He acted, looked, and spoke like a well-educated, highly experienced, confident, but not arrogant man of color. He had it going on. Miss Agnes smiled at her own thoughts. *I bet he has to fight the women off. I feel sorry for his wife.* She shook her head. *Good thing I'm twenty years his senior, at least. I wouldn't let him give me no heart attack.* She giggled.

"What's funny?" Christian glanced at Miss Agnes, sucking her from her naughty thoughts.

She slightly jumped back to her reality at hearing his voice. "Uh, just something I was thinking about. It's nothing," she said, her soft cream skin suddenly turning a rosy red.

He refocused his attention back on the road, pulling to the far right lane and accelerating his speed.

"What else can you tell me about Hezekiah McCoy?" He asked Miss Agnes.

"Only that he's quite a character who has a powerful magnetism about him. Sometimes it's like you can sense the presence of God...or the devil...sometimes I couldn't tell which it was. I do have a hard time seeing him as someone who would take advantage of underage girls, but that's what he was found guilty of. I just don't think that's something he would knowingly do. Then again, I can only go by the man he presents himself to be, which is a powerful orator, a gospel singing preaching and he was the former pastor of Holy Rock which is a mega church in South Memphis, now pastored by his oldest son Khalil McCoy."

"Sounds like you know the man rather well, huh?" he quickly glanced again at Miss Agnes.

She half smiled but remained serious. "I know him because the Reverend Hezekiah McCoy is not new to our firm. He's been a client of our law firm for quite some time. I must admit that some of the things he's accused of that we've represented him on are not always easy to make go away or to win. He has another son who happens to be gay but he's in a traditional marriage. You know man and woman. He has two boys. Pastor McCoy was married for many years to the mother of his two oldest sons. Her name is Fancy McCoy. After they divorced, he got married to the choir director from Holy Rock a couple of years ago. I can tell you, he's definitely no angel."

"Ummm, says a lot," Christian said.

For the next several minutes they maintained silence as he drove along the stretch of highway. Trees and greenery mixed in with hilly land was the scenic tour. One could easily be bored by the uneventful drive. Instead, Christian was enthralled with his own thoughts.

Hezekiah McCoy was one of the top pending cases when Christian arrived at Brachman Law Firm. He had read through the preacher's files which started with the three inch thick manila folder but another box filled with thousands of sheets of papers, depositions, court records, arrest records, and Hezekiah's history. Much of the information had been entered into a file on the computer, but Christian preferred going through the printed papers.

Luna sat with him almost every night, especially on the weekends, helping her husband go through the stacks of papers. While going through the paperwork, and almost at the bottom of the pile, Christian ran across something that piqued his interest. Something struck him as rather odd and hair-raising. He showed the information to Luna.

†

Two nights prior to today's trip, Christian and Luna over dinner talked about Hezekiah McCoy's files. He could count on Luna to be open-minded and to have a good listening ear. He'd found a treasure in Luna and he tried to show her his appreciation every chance he got. She was the epitome of a Proverbs 31 woman and a helpmate.

While they dined out in a Collierville restaurant not far from their home, they talked about their respective new jobs, the people they had met thus far, before turning the conversation to something more pressing; at least it was more of an issue for Christian.

"There's something about Hezekiah McCoy that doesn't sit right with me."

"Like what?"

"I don't know what it is just yet, but the more I went through his files, the more red flags popped up. Not so much about his appeal. I think I've found a loophole that might help me get this dude free. I'm talking about more of his personal life and background. I just keep remembering some things my mother told me."

"Your mother? What does your mother have to do with this?"

"You know how I've been looking for someone who might have known this Franklin fellow or the Bae-bruh dude. All this time I've never met anyone who knew my mother. I'm wondering if this guy might have known her."

"Honey," Luna said reaching across the table and kneading her husband's hand, "I think you're reaching for nothing. There are endless people from Chicago; it's unlikely this McCoy knows your mother or who she slept with back then."

"Maybe I *am* reaching for nothing, and I hear what you're saying, babe, but if there's the slightest possibility, then it would be worth finding out. At least that's what my spirit is telling me. Think about it; he's from Chicago—my mother was from Chicago," Christian said, hesitancy ringing in his voice. "They're around the same age, and from the same area where Mama grew up." Christian removed his hand from the table and from his wife's covering and rubbed his head of thick hair nervously.

"I'm sure it's nothing, honey," she assured him. There was very little she could do when he was in this frame of mind. Luna had come to realize rather than argue with him about how he was grabbing at straws, the more he was set on believing what he wanted to believe.

"Don't let your mind go there, baby. It's not what you think. I'm telling you, just because someone may have, and I'm emphasizing, *may have* lived in the same neighborhood as your mother doesn't mean a thing."

"I'm just saying, I wish I had answers. Mama's dead so I'll never know the full truth."

"Christian, honey, you're making way more out of this than it is. I know you've been in pain ever since your mother told you the truth about your father; but even you said that she was vague about who he is. A nickname like Bae-bruh isn't all that odd. Neither is being from Chicago or attending the same school as your mother. I'm not trying to talk against her; God rest her soul. I can't imagine the weight of keeping a secret like that from you all those years." Luna expressed with a tinge of sadness in her voice.

Christian picked at his flakes of baked flounder repeatedly while shaking his head. Memories of what his mother told him came crowding back like a hidden current.

"You know what, you're right, sweetheart. What was I thinking? I guess I want to find him so bad that I'm seeing things that aren't there."

"I know you want to find him, to know if he's even still alive, but you can't let it consume you. There are too many people walking around who went to the same school or lived in the same neighborhood. That means nothing, baby."

"Yeah, but what if this Hezekiah McCoy fellow knows my mother? Maybe he knew my father too. Maybe he could fill in the missing blanks. What if-—"

"Don't do this to yourself, Christian—not again. You've been, no *we've* been," she corrected, "searching for your birth father for years. Every time you got your hopes up, thinking maybe you had found a clue or met someone who knew him or your mother-—"

Christian played with his food while intently listening to Luna. "Only to meet another brick wall," he finished her sentence.

She reached across the table and caressed his hand. "Baby, we're in a new city, we have new careers, and we're financially blessed. I mean, God has been good to us. Remember what His word says in Philippians: Forget what lies behind and strain forward to what lies ahead. In simple words, let the past be the past," she said tenderly.

Christian looked at his wife. His pain was on full display on his face but the words she spoke somehow soothed his spirit.

"Charles Black was your father. Maybe not by blood, but you've said so many times ever since I've known you that no matter who your birth father that Charles Black would be the only man worthy to be called "Dad."

Christian nodded. He heard the words his wife spoke, but for some reason he couldn't push away the thoughts swirling in his mind of finding his father. Why was he suddenly drawn to this Hezekiah McCoy dude? Something was troubling him about McCoy and he hadn't even met the guy yet.

Luna looked at her husband and caressed the side of his face. "I wish you wouldn't keep doing this to yourself." The pain in his eyes was unmistakable. She wanted desperately to help him find the answers he longed for, but like all the other times before when he would start this mad search, she didn't know if she could.

The chase for his birth father always lead to a dead end. She had experienced similar scenarios many times with him during their marriage when just hearing someone came from Chicago and lived in or near the same neighborhood as his mother, would send him into another unproductive search that reopened wounds that had never fully healed in his life. He would then sink into a depression for days, sometimes even weeks afterward. She didn't want that to happen again.

They had just moved to Memphis, and already he had started up again. She prayed he would leave well enough alone, yet something within told her he would not.

thirty

"Be strong enough to face the world each day. Be weak enough to know you cannot do everything alone." Unknown

Hezekiah traipsed around the prison grounds, chest poked out, muscles bulging, and a scowl on his face. He'd done three hours of strenuous work out on the overcrowded prison yard. Today he was expecting a visit from his newly appointed lawyer. He hoped that dude was as good as he heard he was.

He strolled confidently off the yard and headed inside toward his pod. Taking advantage of being alone inside his cell, he retrieved his cell phone and called Xavier.

No answer. Next, he called Stiles.

"Hey, there," Stiles answered. "How's it going, Preacher Man?"

"It's all good. Hey, have you seen Xavier? I just called him but he didn't answer. My new attorney is supposed to be coming up here later today. I wanted to check with Xavier to see if there was anything about the financial arrangements I needed to discuss."

"If you're concerned about his payment, nothing's changed. It'll still be handled by the church, and me, if necessary. So don't worry about that. It's all covered."

Hezekiah exhaled. "'Preciate that. God is good to me even in spite of all I've done."

"Don't go there. We're thinking good thoughts, blessed thoughts. Let the past go," Stiles encouraged. "You asked for his forgiveness, now forgive yourself."

"You're right. What's the latest on Rianna?" He changed the subject.

"Last I spoke to her, which was day before yesterday, she was getting ready to move back to Apartment 3D. We're handling all her moving expenses and making sure she gets special transportation to take her from Lion's Gate back to her apartment. Her friend, uh, Tiny, is supposed to be with her. We gave her a little something for helping out."

"Good, good," Hezekiah said, satisfied things were going his way. "I didn't think she would accept the counter offers but hey, she signed off on everything, except for those two credit cards. But at least that was reduced to three grand instead of the five she was haggling for. I can live with that."

"Yeah, it was worth it to get her to sign those papers," Stiles agreed.

"Man, I can't believe I'm officially legally *single*. The alimony is still being negotiated, but even with that, it's not for the seven years she was going for and it's definitely not for the amount she wanted."

"I know right. You came out on top if you ask me," said Stiles.

Hezekiah chuckled. "Just a few more things to work out behind the scenes and it'll all be over."

"You should feel good. Things are going in your favor, and this is only the beginning. I believe that Christian Black fellow is going to get things moving on your behalf. I got that feeling," Stiles said, smiling over the phone.

"Okay, if you say so, and like we both know, there's nothing too hard for God. I have to remind myself of that every now and then."

†

"I don't know why but I believe this new lawyer is going to be the one to get Hezekiah a new trial. He's going to do something. I can feel it."

"I hope you're right, Ma. At least maybe he can get his sentence shortened," Xavier said as he, Pepper, Khalil, Eliana and their kids, along with Fancy enjoyed a small family cookout in Khalil's backyard.

"I'm here," Victoria said, appearing at the back gate.

Xavier ran up to his mother-in-law and removed the large aluminum pan covered in foil out of her arms.

"Be careful. It's hot. It's my famous spaghetti and three-cheese casserole. I have some rolls and sodas in the car. Oh, and a peach cobbler is out there too."

"Whoa, that sounds good," said Pepper. "Thanks, Mom."

"I'll go get it," Khalil offered and ran up to stand next to his brother.

Victoria gave him the keys she held in her hand. "Thanks, guys."

As the children played on the play pad in the backyard, the grownups sat around under the covered lanai. The weather was seasonably warm but comfortable; a fair indication after a rather light winter, spring was forthcoming.

Stiles appeared next.

Khalil and Xavier ran toward him and greeted him, helping him with Pastor and Josie as he led them inside the back yard.

Pastor wore a look of bewilderment but then he broke out in a smile when he saw tables full of food, especially the trays of sweets.

Fancy went up and hugged Josie and led her to a seat.

"It's so good to have you and Pastor here," Fancy beamed.

"I'm glad we could make it. It's not always easy to get Pastor to go out the house these days—unless I tell him we're going to church. Then he's raring to go." She and Fancy laughed as Fancy guided her over to the outdoor sofa.

Stiles led Pastor to a chair next to Josie. They had to speak extra loud because Pastor's hearing wasn't so good and he kept losing his hearing aids.

All in all, a good time was being had by all. Gathered around eating and drinking, they laughed and joked as one big happy family. Sometimes the conversation turned serious and other times it was light and happy.

"I missed a call from Dad earlier today. I was at the gym working out. He left me a voicemail. Said he would hit me back up when he could, but he did say his new lawyer was supposed to be there later today. He may already be up there by now," Xavier shared. "Overall, he sounded good, his voice was strong, didn't sound stressed or anything."

"That's a blessing," said Fancy, sighing and taking a swallow of her freshly squeezed lemonade. "Eliana," she said, looking over her shoulder, "you know you make the best lemonade," she complimented, taking another swallow.

Eliana grinned. "Thank you, Fancy."

They all greeted Victoria as she approached.

Fancy patted the space next to her. "Over here," she told Victoria.

"Okay. Let me fix my plate and I'll be over there."

Khalil reappeared with the remaining food and drink items. This was what life was about.

Fancy's heart was overjoyed at the sight of her family. Through all the hardships, changes, and the unpredictability of life, their family was still together. Her cell phone buzzed. She looked at the screen. Tears welled in her eyes and tiny splatters spilled onto her phone when she viewed her *Word for the Day* app. She'd been using the daily vocabulary app ever since Victoria suggested it a few months ago. Today's word happened to be *redemption: the action of saving or being saved from sin, error, or evil.*

She quickly got up, moved away from the crowd, and settled under a towering oak tree in the backyard. "Redemption," she said under her breath. Her mind went into spiritual overdrive. The master had a plan for her family and for Holy Rock. Thinking back, she recalled Xavier's outburst during one of his visits a little over a year ago. "*I'm gay, I'm miserable in this marriage. I love my boys, Ma, and I care about Pepper, but...*" Battling those unnatural desires that send men into ruin had him in a fight for his life. She looked over at Xavier and wiped away tears with her hand. She watched him playing with his sons and smiled at the loving sight. *Lord, he's trying.*

Next, she shifted her attention to her eldest son, Khalil, and a recent conversation they'd had. *"Ma, I'm a grown man, Detria ain't nothing but a trick. I could never be serious about somebody like her." Khalil laughed and brushed her off when she tried to warn him about her and the bad example he was setting for youth in the congregation.* His adultery with Detria almost destroyed his marriage but fatherhood had opened his eyes to the importance of family and walking a righteous path. She watched from afar as Khalil cradled his baby girl and planted kisses on her forehead.

Tears streamed down her cheeks as Fancy thought about Hezekiah. *Lord, somebody tell me what this man has that makes me care when I don't want to care.* All the stunts he had pulled in the past had seemingly caught up with him. According to what Stiles had told her, including his divorcing Rianna, she believed Hezekiah McCoy, without a doubt, was leaving his old ways behind and becoming the man God had called him to be.

Fancy smiled, while inwardly thanking God for everything he had done and was doing in the Graham and McCoy families. This was certainly a time of redemption and forgiveness, a time to move in the path and will God had for each of them. Fellowshipping with family, friends, and loved ones in spite of the hardships and the upsets of life. The ties that bind proved to be strong and unbreakable. Redeeming the times. Forgetting the faults and failures of the past. Enjoying life one moment, one day, one minute at a time. Fancy lifted her eyes heavenward and whispered as she returned to her seat, "Thank you, Lord for redeeming Holy Rock."

Words from the Author

~Redeeming Holy Rock~

This series keeps revealing so much to me each and every time I write the next installment. Just when I think things are about to change for the good between the McCoy's and the Graham's, life throws another curveball. But isn't that the way it is in REAL LIFE? Just when we think everything is going our way, or things have changed for the better, something can come soaring into our lives and disrupt everything.

The McCoys and the Grahams are no different from people like you and me. They just happen to be in a story book! We are all in need of redemption in some way, shape, form, or fashion. The imperfections of life, mixed with its good times, not so good times, and everything in between can throw us for a loop. We sometimes make choices that don't always prove to be wise. Other times we flounder and flail. But we also prosper and prevail. The art is not in falling but in making every effort to get up and not stay down. When we know there is an out, when we know that we can change our circumstances and make things new, redemption becomes even more necessary and essential.

As I start to bring this dynamic family saga [My Son's Wife series] to a close, remember that life may not always deal the exact hand you expect or hope for. However, keep in mind with positive thinking, self-affirmations combined with faith in the Most High, you can overcome what you may have thought were insurmountable obstacles. You may not be able to climb *every* mountain but like the people in this series, you may very well learn how to *go around* them or even *through* many of them. You can be redeemed, restored, and renewed!

So be encouraged; enjoy reading and thank you for traveling this literary journey along with me. Remember, I write "*Perfect Stories About Imperfect People Like You....and Me!*"

Until the next perfect story about imperfect people like you....and me!

Shelia E. Bell
God's amazing girl!

More Perfect Stories About Imperfect People Like You...and Me

SHELIA E. BELL

My Son's Wife Series

My Son's Wife: The Beginning (Book 1)
My Son's Ex-Wife: Aftershock (Book 2)
My Son's Next Wife (Book 3)
My Sister My Momma My Wife (Book 4)
My Wife My Baby...And Him (Book 5)
The McCoy's of Holy Rock (Book 6)
Dem McCoy Boys (Book 7)
My Brother, Father...And Me (Book 8)
My Truth, My Time, My Turn (Book 9)
Dem Folk at Holy Rock (Book 10)
Thicker Than Water (Book 11)
Redeeming Holy Rock (12)
Whom the Sons Set Free (13)

Holy Rock Chronicles

(My Son's Wife short story spin-off)

Calling Dr. Daniels (1)
The Woman in Apartment 3D (2)
Ruthless Rianna (3)

Holy Rock Chronicles

(My Son's Wife short story spin-off)

Christian Black, Esq. (4)
If the Price is Right (5)

Love Shoulda Brought You Home (6)

Adverse City Series

The Real Housewives of Adverse City 1

The Real Housewives of Adverse City 2

The Real Housewives of Adverse City 3

The Real Housewives of Adverse City 4

Beautiful Ugly 2-book series

Beautiful Ugly

True Beauty

Young Adult Titles

House of Cars

The Life of Payne

The Lollipop Girl

Standalone Novels

Show A Little Love 1 & 2 (*out of print*)

Always Now and Forever Love Hurts

Into Each Life

Sinsatiable

What's Blood Got To Do With It?

Only In My Dreams

The House Husband

Cross Road

Forever Ain't Enough

Anthologies

Bended Knees

Weary to Will
Learning to Love Me
Show A Little Love (1)

Nonfiction
A Christian's Perspective: Journey Through Grief
How to Live Your Life Like It's Golden

Journals
Journal Your Way Through It
Sister Sister Book Log Journal

Contact information
www.sheliaebell.net
www.sheliawritesbooks.com
sheliawritesbooks@yahoo.com
www.facebook.com/sheliawritesbooks
@sheliaebell (Twitter & Instagram)

Please join my mailing list
for literary updates and new book release information
www.sheliawritesbooks.com

If you enjoyed this book or any of my books, please go to your favorite review site and leave a positive review!

Other links to my books
bit.ly/sheliaebell
bit.ly/sheliabn
bit.ly/sheliabell

www.sheliawritesbooks.com

#iwriteforfilmandtv
#iwritebestsellers
#iwritepageturners
#iwritenewyorktimesbestsellers
#iamgodsamazinggirl

Perfect Stories About Imperfect People Like You ...and Me!

Made in the USA
Middletown, DE
12 August 2022

71209838R00177